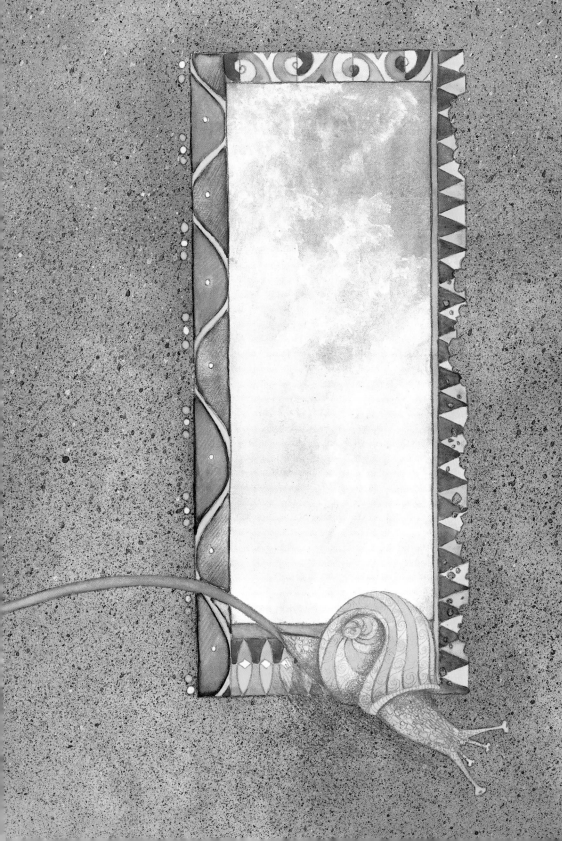

This book
belongs
to

. . . .

ACC CHILDREN'S CLASSICS

an imprint of
Antique Collectors' Club Ltd
5 Church Street, Woodbridge,
Suffolk IP12 1DS, UK
—— and ——
Market Street Industrial Park, Wappingers' Falls,
NY 12590, USA

This edition of *Granny's Wonderful Chair*
first published 1999

ISBN 1 85149 706 4

Illustrations © Gisèle Rime, 1999

The moral rights of the illustrator have been asserted.

British Library Cataloguing-in-Publication Data
A catalogue record for this book is available from the British Library

Published and printed in England
on Consort Royal Satin paper
from Donside Mills, Aberdeen
by Antique Collectors' Club Ltd.

FRANCES BROWNE

Introduction by
FRANCES HODGSON BURNETT

GRANNY'S WONDERFUL CHAIR

Illustrated by
GISÈLE RIME

ACC CHILDREN'S CLASSICS

CONTENTS

THE STORY OF THE LOST FAIRY BOOK

Through all the years of my life this has been my Fairy Book. All the other Fairy Books belong to thousands of other people, but this one is mine, and though thousands of children may begin now to read it, I shall always feel that it belongs to me and that they have only borrowed it from me.

There was something mysterious about it. When I was five or six years old and went to a tiny school which was kept by two daughters of an old clergyman, there one day happened to me a most beautiful thing. It appeared that I had been a good child throughout all that part of my career presided over by Miss Alice and Miss Mary. To my great pride Miss Mary and Miss Alice told me so, and even added that, as a reward for my excellent conduct, they intended to present me with a prize. The prize was to be a story book, as I cared more for story books than for the thrones of Kings and crowns of Queens. Across all the years which have passed since then I can look back to-day and see the little square school-room up-stairs in the clergyman's house, and at a window which looked over green fields with hawthorn hedges round them, I can see the very little girl who leaned against the window ledge and quaked with joy as she looked at Miss Mary, who was telling her this stupendously delightful thing. In those days little girls only received presents of books upon solemn and exalting occasions, and this little girl had so few that she was obliged to tell to herself – in whispers – the stories she wanted to hear.

"Alice and I went out together and bought it, Frances dear," Miss Mary said with a doubtful air, "but we had not time to look at it when we were in the shop. And I am afraid it is a very silly book. It is all about fairies."

The very little girl leaning against the window felt her cheeks growing red with all sorts of feelings, but principally with guilty joy. A book about fairies had not happened to her before, and her conscience smote her (being a very large conscience for such a little girl) for the thrill of delight which ran all over her from the toes of her ankle strap shoes to the ends of her hair. To be so rejoiced over a silly book all about fairies was plainly not conduct worthy of a little girl who was receiving a prize for meritorious behaviour.

"Alice and I thought of sending it back to the shop after we found out about it," said Miss Mary (and then the little girl almost fell into a small round heap of woe upon the floor), "but we found we had no time and so decided that we would give it to you. It may not be quite as silly as it looked. So here it is."

It was a little green book with gilt decorations upon it, and it was called:

Granny's Wonderful Chair

and on the blank page at the beginning were written these flattering lines:

"To Miss Frances Hodgson,
From Mary and Alice Hague, as a reward
for politeness and good behaviour."

The next thing that I remember is that little girl poring over the book in corners of her nursery, in nooks in the garden, in any quiet place where one could sit down on the grass, on stairs, on a chair or a footstool. In the hours in which she opened the leaves of *Granny's Wonderful Chair* she wandered into a strange and beautiful country which was like no other country she had heard or dreamed of before, or has had the good fortune to travel into at any time since. The first sentence she read told her that it belonged to "An old-time long ago, when fairies were in the world." This was a joy in itself. Other books always spoke of a time when people *believed* in fairies, but this one told of the days when fairies were in the world. So one had no need to doubt anything or think it was only a pretence. In all the stories fairies were spoken of, not as if they were unreal creatures quite different from anyone else, but as if they were as real as birds and butterflies and little children. They made part of the crowds which went to festivities; they danced on the hilltops in countries they liked; they went away when people grew cross and their countries dull, and they came back to their old places, when everyone became happy and good-tempered and the countries were bright again. They went to fairs with other people quite comfortably and they sat spinning on silver spinning-wheels at cottage firesides when everyone was asleep. They came and went and were part of the populace, and one felt one might meet one at any moment. The chief little girl in the book – her name was Snowflower – lived "on the edge of a great forest in a little cottage built of peat and thatched with reeds. Tall trees sheltered it, swallows built in the eaves, and daisies grew thick about the door." The words had such a beautiful sound when one read them aloud to one's self, and the cottage seemed so real, nestling on the edge of the great forest, which was so deep – so deep – that there could be no world beyond it.

That was the charm of this country. The forests were so deep, the moorlands stretched so far, the hills sloped up to the very sky, and one knew they were lost in the red sunset clouds. There was no boundary to anywhere. There were no places where things ended, "Long ago when the Fairies were in the world;" one wandered on, and on, and on, until one met a story and stopped to live in it. This was the world the small reader of the book wandered into when she began to read the first page, and she has never quite left it since.

I do not know how long she lived with the book, reading its stories over and over, carrying it about in her hand, sleeping with it under her pillow and seeking her fortune in the Beautiful Country in her sleep. It seemed to her that it was her friend for years. But at last came the Mystery. The book was gone – quite gone. It did not seem to be lost as things usually are. No one had seen it for any "last time." No search would find it. Everybody looked, everybody asked questions, but there was no clue, no trace; the little book had disappeared, not only from the nursery, not only from the house, but as it seemed, from the very world.

Then the little girl told herself a story which was a sort of comfort to her. This was what she used to whisper to herself about it:

"It was really a fairy book. The fairies put it on the counter of the book shop in Manchester for Miss Mary and Miss Alice to buy for me. They wanted a little girl like me to have it. No doubt they were hiding behind things on the shelves in the shop and peeping out when Miss Mary asked how much it cost. Perhaps they danced all the way home with them and were in the school-room when it was given to me. When Miss Mary thought of sending it back to the shop because it was about them and she thought them silly, perhaps one of them flew upon her shoulder and whispered in her ear and told her that they were quite as real as she was and were not silly at all. Perhaps they have been dancing round me all the time I have been reading about them, and they have liked me because

I was so fond of them and knew they were really true. But it was their particular book, and after I had read all the stories so many times they knew some other little girl who needed it, and so they just took it away to fairy land and made it new again, and then carried it to another book shop and watched until it was bought for her. It was not a shop book – it was a fairy book. It was only lent to me."

And she always liked to think of the coming and going of the Lost Fairy Book.

But she had not lost the Beautiful Country. She knew it too well. On the wide heath covered with purple bloom she could wander whensoever she chose; on the broad pasture carpeted with violets, she could sit and watch the thousands of snow-white sheep and hear the old man playing his pipe; in the grove of great rose trees she could lie and listen to the thousands of nightingales as they sang, and in the deep, deep forests which reached to the end of the world, she could lose herself in the green shadows and know that the fairies were dancing on the velvet moss and hanging on the ferns. She never lost the Beautiful Country and she never will.

But as she grew older and had many things to write and much work to do, the stories faded somewhat. She could not quite remember what happened to the two shepherds when they roamed after their wandering flock, the things Merrymind did in Dame Dreary's land became rather indistinct, she was not really sure of all that occurred when Civil the young fisherman was drawn down through the water by "the tallest, stateliest ladies he had ever seen," and lived with them and their strange people through twelve months feasting in the splendid caves beneath the sea. She could remember the moorlands and the dells where tiny men and women danced, attired in russet and green, but the details of their doings drifted away from her. When she grew into a young woman she wanted so much to recall them again quite clearly that she made up her mind to find a copy of the Lost Fairy Book somewhere if it was to be found by searching for it. So she used to go into book shops in different countries and ask if anyone had one for sale, or if anyone knew anything of the existence of such a book and could tell her where it might be bought. But no one ever knew. She inquired in libraries, she asked people both in England and America, but no one seemed ever to have heard of it – it was a Lost Fairy Book indeed. But when she was married and had two little boys of her own she used to try to call back from her nursery days such fragments as she could remember of the lovely happenings to Fairyfoot and Merrymind and the Lords of the White and Grey Castles, and she would weave them into something complete enough to tell when stories were very much wanted. She told them to other children as well as to her own, and they were always beloved and everyone wished he or she could find the Lost Fairy Book. But for years and years, and years, and years – and also for years, and years more than that – no one ever did.

But in time the Fairies did not wish their book to be lost any longer; in fact, they intended it to be found, so that other children should wander in the forests and on the purple heath. So they invented something, as fairies always can. This was what they invented.

There was a little girl in Boston who had been promised that she should be told the story of Prince Fairyfoot. Time went so fast and so many things happened that after months the story had not been told, and the First Owner of the Lost Fairy Book had gone away from Boston town. And as a promise made to a little girl or a little boy is a very unbreakable thing, the First Owner felt this one lie heavy on her conscience and she made a plan to redeem it. She gathered together from the shadowy places in her mind all she could recall of Prince Fairyfoot; to make it complete she invented new fairies and filled in the blank places with new things, trying all the time to make the story feel as much like the old one as possible. She wrote it out on note paper, made a pretty cover of pale pink and pale blue satin ornamented with illuminated letters, edged and tied it with a silver cord, and sent it to the little girl as an Easter greeting. Then she felt she had kept her promise and was not a dishonourable person any longer.

This was of course really a thing invented by the fairies, which is proved by the fact that through this very thing their book was found again.

The little girl liked the story very much. She was so delighted with it that the First Owner, who had rewritten it, thought it would be a pleasure to try to rewrite the others. This she had not time to do more than merely think of that year, but some time later, when the editor of a certain children's magazine wanted some stories very much, she remembered the Easter greeting again. No doubt the fairies sprang upon her shoulder and reminded her and told her what she must do. What she did was to write to the editor and tell her about the beloved Lost Fairy Book. "I have not seen it since I was a little girl," she wrote. "No one but myself seems to know anything about it, but when I tell the stories to children they always love them. What do you think of this idea? Suppose I were to try and rewrite all I can remember, fill in the forgotten places as well as I can, and let you publish the series under the title of 'Stories from the Lost Fairy Book. Retold by the Child who read them.'"

The editor was very much pleased with this, and so it was agreed that the stories were to be rewritten as soon as the First Owner had time. The story of Fairyfoot, being already written, was sent ahead. It happened, however, that time could never be found to write the rest. So after a good many months Fairyfoot was published. As the editor was in England the First Owner's letter about the Lost Fairy Book was laid away and forgotten and so, by mistake, the story was published without the title, which explained that it was not a new story but an old one told over again. This of course was what the fairies intended when they made their plan for giving their book again to the children. The story in the magazine was read by some one who really owned an old copy of the Lost Fairy Book. Perhaps it was the very one which had disappeared so mysteriously so many years ago. I think it was. The lady who owned it naturally loved it very much and thought it was her special fairy book, just as I felt it was mine. When she saw Fairyfoot retold in the magazine with additions and alterations, she no doubt felt wronged and robbed. She wrote to inquire how it happened that *her* Fairyfoot was given to the public this way. The editor of the magazine explained to her and told her about the First Owner's letter and the title which should have been added and how it was forgotten. And so the Lost Fairy Book was found and the fairies did what they had planned to do.

The spell which had seemed laid upon it was broken. Almost immediately even I who had so long searched for it, found an old copy in a second-hand book shop in London.

Since then I have never travelled in any country or across any sea without carrying it with me. I like to read it to grown-up people who have never known anything of wide heaths and purple bloom and the piping of shepherds from the tops of hills. They like to lose themselves in the Beautiful Country and I have never found one who really wanted to leave it and come back. I never want to come back myself.

I do not know why the Lost Fairy Book was lost so long, but I do know it was not found again for nothing. And now I feel as if I was lending the book, which has always been mine, to other children who will wander in the forests which reach to the end of the world.

But it is really *my* Fairy Book.

From an introduction written by
Frances Hodgson Burnett in 1904

Chapter 1

INTRODUCTORY

In an old time, long ago, when the fairies were in the world, there lived a little girl so uncommonly fair and pleasant of look, that they called her Snowflower. This girl was good as well as pretty. No one had ever seen her frown or heard her say a cross word, and young and old were glad when they saw her coming.

Snowflower had no relation in the world but a very old grandmother, called Dame Frostyface; people did not like her quite so well as her grand-daughter, for she was cross enough at times, but always kind to Snowflower; and they lived together in a little cottage built of peat and thatched with reeds, on the edge of a great forest. Tall trees sheltered its back from the north wind, the midday sun made its front warm and cheerful swallows built in the eaves and daisies grew thick at the door; but there were none in all that country poorer than Snowflower and her grandmother. A cat and two hens were all their livestock: their bed was dry grass, and the only good piece of furniture in the cottage was a great armchair with wheels on its feet, a black velvet cushion, and many curious carvings of flowers and fawns on its dark oaken back.

On that chair Dame Frostyface sat spinning from morning till night to maintain herself and her granddaughter, while Snowflower gathered sticks for firing, looked after the hens and the cat, and did whatever else her grandmother bade her. There was nobody in the shire could spin such fine yarn as Dame Frostyface, but she spun very slowly. Her wheel was as old as herself and far the more worn; indeed the wonder was that it did not fall to pieces. So the dame's earnings were small and their living meagre. Snowflower, however, felt no want of good dinners or fine clothes. Every evening, when the fire was heaped with the sticks she had gathered till it blazed and crackled up the cottage chimney, Dame Frostyface set aside her wheel and told her a new story.

Often did the little girl wonder where her grandmother had gathered so many stories, but she soon learned that. One sunny morning, at the time of the swallows coming, the dame rose up, put on the grey hood and mantle in which she carried her yarn to the fairs, and said: 'My child, I am going a long journey to visit an aunt of mine, who lives far in the north country. I cannot take you with me because my aunt is the crossest woman alive and never liked young people; but the hens will lay eggs for you, there is barley-meal in the barrel, and as you have been a good girl I'll tell you what to do when you feel lonely. Lay your head gently down on the cushion of the armchair, and say: "Chair of my grandmother, tell me a story." It was made by a cunning fairy who lived in the forest when I was young, and she gave it to me because she knew nobody could keep what they got hold of better. Remember, you must never ask a story more than once in the day; and if there be any occasion to travel, you have only to seat yourself in it and say: "Chair of my grandmother, take me such a way." It will carry you wherever you wish; but mind to oil the wheels before you set out, for I have sat on it these forty years in that same corner.'

Having said this, Dame Frostyface set forth to see her aunt in the north country. Snowflower gathered firing and looked after the hens and cat as usual. She baked herself a cake or two of the barley-meal; but when the evening fell the cottage looked lonely. Then Snowflower remembered her grandmother's words, and laying her head gently down she said: 'Chair of my grandmother, tell me a story.'

Scarce were the words spoken when a clear voice from under the velvet cushion began to tell a new and most wonderful tale, which surprised Snowflower so much that she forgot to be frightened. After that the good girl was lonely no more. Every morning she baked a barley cake, and every evening the chair told her a new story; but she could never find out who owned the voice, though Snowflower showed her gratitude by polishing up the oaken back and dusting the velvet cushion, till the chair looked as good as new. The swallows came and built in the eaves, the daisies grew thicker than ever at the door; but great misfortunes fell upon Snowflower. Notwithstanding all her care, she forgot to clip the hens' wings, and they flew away one morning to visit their friends, the pheasants, who lived far in the forest; the cat followed them to see its relations; the barley-meal was eaten up, except a couple of handfuls; and Snowflower had often strained her eyes in hopes of seeing the grey mantle, but there was no appearance of Dame Frostyface.

'My grandmother stays long,' said Snowflower to herself, 'and by and by there will be nothing to eat. If I could get to her, perhaps she would advise me what to do; and this is a good occasion for travelling.'

Next day at sunrise Snowflower oiled the chair's wheels, baked a cake out of the last of the meal, took it in her lap by way of provision for the journey, seated herself and said: 'Chair of my grandmother, take me the way she went.'

Presently the chair gave a creak and began to move out of the cottage and into the forest the very way Dame Frostyface had taken, where it rolled along at the rate of a coach and six. Snowflower was amazed at this style of travelling, but the chair never stopped nor stayed the whole summer day, till as the sun was setting they came upon an open space where a hundred men were hewing down the tall trees with their axes, a hundred more were cleaving them for firewood, and twenty wagoners, with horses and wagons, were carrying the wood away. 'O chair of my grandmother, stop!' said Snowflower, for she was tired and also wished to know what this might mean. The chair immediately stood still, and Snowflower, seeing an old woodcutter who looked civil, stepped up to him and said: 'Good father, tell me why you cut all this wood?'

'What ignorant country girl are you?' replied the man, 'not to have heard of the great feast which our sovereign, King Winwealth, means to give on the birthday of his only daughter, the Princess Greedalind? It will last seven days. Everybody will be feasted and this wood is to roast the oxen and the sheep, the geese and the turkeys, amongst whom there is a great lamentation throughout the land.'

When Snowflower heard that, she could not help wishing to see and perhaps share in such a noble feast, after living so long on barley cakes; so seating herself she said: 'Chair of my grandmother, take me quickly to the palace of King Winwealth.'

The words were hardly spoken when off the chair started through the trees and out of the forest to the great amazement of the woodcutters, who, never having seen such a sight before, threw down their axes, left their wagons and followed Snowflower to the gates of a great and splendid city, fortified with strong walls and high towers, and standing in the midst of a wide plain covered with cornfields, orchards and villages.

It was the richest city in all the land; merchants from every quarter came there to buy and sell, and there was a saying that people had only to live seven years in it to make their fortunes. Rich as they were, however, Snowflower thought she had never seen so many discontented, covetous faces as looked out from the great shops, grand houses and fine coaches, when her chair rattled along the streets; indeed the citizens did not stand high in repute for either good nature or honesty. But it had not been so when King Winwealth was young, and he and his brother, Prince Wisewit, governed the land together. Wisewit was a wonderful prince for knowledge and prudence; he knew the whole art of government, the tempers of men and the powers of the stars; moreover he was a great magician, and it was said of him that he could never die or grow old. In his time there was neither discontent nor sickness in the city – strangers were hospitably entertained without price or questions. Lawsuits there were none, and no one locked his door at night. The fairies used to come there at May Day and Michaelmas, for they were Prince Wisewit's friends – all but one, called Fortunetta, a shortsighted but very cunning fairy, who hated everybody wiser than herself, and the prince especially, because she could never deceive him.

There was peace and pleasure for many a year in King Winwealth's city, till one day at midsummer Prince Wisewit went alone to the forest, in search of a strange herb for his garden, and he never came back; and though the king with all his guards searched far and near, no news was ever heard of him. When his brother was gone, King Winwealth grew lonely in his great palace, so he married a certain princess called Wantall and brought her home to be his queen. This princess was neither handsome nor agreeable. People thought she must have gained the king's love by enchantment, for her whole dowry was a desert island with a huge pit in it that never could be filled, and her disposition was so covetous that the more she got the greedier she grew. In process of time the king and queen had an only daughter, who was to be the heiress of all their dominions. Her name was the Princess Greedalind, and the whole city was making preparations to celebrate her birthday – not that they cared much for the princess, who was remarkably like her mother both in looks and temper, but as she was King Winwealth's only daughter, people came from far and near to the festival, and among them strangers and fairies who had not been there since the day of Prince Wisewit.

There was surprising bustle about the palace – a most noble building, so spacious that it had a room for every day in the year. All the floors were of ebony and all the ceilings of silver, and there was such a supply of golden dishes used by the household, that five hundred armed men kept guard night and day lest any of them should be stolen. When these guards saw Snowflower and her chair, they ran one after the other to tell the king, for the like had never been seen nor heard of in his dominions, and the whole court crowded out to see the little maiden and her chair that came of itself.

When Snowflower saw the lords and ladies in their embroidered robes and splendid jewels, she began to feel ashamed of her own bare feet and linen gown; but at length taking courage, she answered all their questions and told them everything about her wonderful chair. The queen and the princess cared for nothing that was not gilt. The courtiers had learned the same fashion and all turned away in high disdain except the old king, who, thinking the chair might amuse him sometimes when he got out of spirits, allowed Snowflower to stay and feast with the scullion in his worst kitchen. The poor little girl was glad of any quarters, though nobody made her welcome – even the servants despised her bare feet and linen gown. They would give her chair no room but in a dusty corner behind the back door, where Snowflower was told she might sleep at night and eat up the scraps the cook threw away.

That very day the feast began; it was fine to see the multitudes of coaches and people on foot and on horseback who crowded to the palace and filled every room according to their rank. Never had Snowflower seen such roasting and boiling. There was wine for the lords and spiced ale for the common people, music and dancing of all kinds, and the best of gay dresses; but with all the good cheer there seemed little merriment and a deal of ill humour in the palace.

Some of the guests thought they should have been feasted in grander rooms; others were vexed to see many finer than themselves. All the servants were dissatisfied because they did not get presents. There was somebody caught every hour stealing the cups, and a multitude of people were always at the gates clamouring for goods and lands which Queen Wantall had taken from them. The guards continually drove them away, but they came back again and could be heard plainly in the highest banquet hall: so it was not wonderful that the old king's spirits got uncommonly low that evening after supper. His favourite page, who always stood behind him, perceiving this, reminded his majesty of the little girl and her chair.

'It is a good thought,' said King Winwealth. 'I have not heard a story this many a year. Bring the child and the chair instantly!'

The favourite page sent a message to the first kitchen who told the master cook, the master cook told the kitchen-maid, the kitchen-maid told the chief scullion, the chief scullion told the dust boy and he told Snowflower to wash her face, rub up her chair and go to the highest banquet hall, for the great King Winwealth wished to hear a story.

Nobody offered to help her, but when she had made herself as smart as she could with soap and water, and rubbed the chair till it looked as if dust had never fallen on it, she seated herself and said: 'Chair of my grandmother, take me to the highest banquet hall.'

Instantly the chair marched in a grave and courtly fashion out of the kitchen, up the grand staircase and into the highest hall. The chief lords and ladies of the land were entertained there, besides many fairies and notable people from distant countries. There had never been such company in the palace since the time of Prince Wisewit; nobody wore less than embroidered satin. King Winwealth sat on his ivory throne in a robe of purple velvet, stiff with flowers of gold; the queen sat by his side in a robe of silver cloth, clasped with pearls; but the Princess Greedalind was finer still, the feast being in her honour. She wore a robe of cloth of gold, clasped with diamonds; two

waiting-ladies in white satin stood, one on either side, to hold her fan and handkerchief; and two pages, in gold-lace livery, stood behind her chair. With all that Princess Greedalind looked ugly and spiteful; she and her mother were angry to see a barefooted girl and an old chair allowed to enter the banquet hall.

The supper table was still covered with golden dishes and the best of good things, but no one offered Snowflower a morsel: so, having made a humble curtsy to the king, the queen, the princess and the good company, most of whom scarcely noticed her, the poor little girl sat down upon the carpet, laid her head on the velvet cushion as she used to do in the old cottage and said: 'Chair of my grandmother, tell me a story.'

Everybody was astonished – even to the angry queen and the spiteful princess – when a clear voice from under the cushion said: 'Listen to the story of the Christmas Cuckoo!'

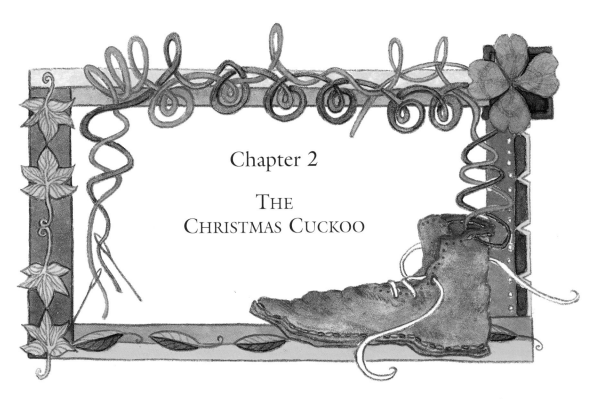

Chapter 2

THE CHRISTMAS CUCKOO

Once upon a time there stood in the midst of a bleak moor, in the north country, a certain village. All its inhabitants were poor, for their fields were barren and they had little trade; but the poorest of them all were two brothers called Scrub and Spare, who followed the cobbler's craft and had but one stall between them. It was a hut built of clay and wattles. The door was low and always open by day, for there was no window. The roof did not entirely keep out the rain and the only thing comfortable about it was a wide hearth, for which the brothers could never find wood enough to make a sufficient fire. There they worked in most brotherly friendship, though with little encouragement.

The people of that village were not extravagant in shoes, and better cobblers than Scrub and Spare might be found. Spiteful people said there were no shoes so bad that they would not be worse for their mending. Nevertheless Scrub and Spare managed to live between their own trade, a small barley-field and a cottage garden, till one unlucky day when a new cobbler arrived in the village. He had lived in the capital city of the kingdom, and by his own account cobbled for the queen and the princesses. His awls were sharp, his lasts were new; he set up his stall in a neat cottage with two windows. The villagers soon found out that one patch of his would wear two of the brothers'. In short, all the mending left Scrub and Spare and went to the new cobbler. The season had been wet and cold, their barley did not ripen well and the cabbages never half closed in the garden. So the brothers were poor that winter, and when Christmas came they had nothing to feast on but a barley loaf, a piece of rusty bacon and some small beer of their own brewing. Worse than that, the snow was very deep and they could get no firewood. Their hut stood at the end of the village and beyond it spread the bleak moor, now all white and silent; but that moor had once been a forest and great roots of old trees were still to be found in it, loosened from the soil and laid bare by the winds and rains – one of these, a rough, gnarled log, lay hard by their door, the half of it above the snow, and Spare said to his brother:

'Shall we sit here cold on Christmas while the great root lies yonder? Let us chop it up for firewood; the work will make us warm.'

'No,' said Scrub; 'it's not right to chop wood on Christmas; besides, that root is too hard to be broken with any hatchet.'

'Hard or not we must have a fire,' replied Spare. 'Come, brother, help me in with it. Poor as we are, there is nobody in the village will have such a yule log as ours.'

Scrub liked a little grandeur, and in hopes of having a fine yule log both brothers strained and strove with all their might till, between pulling and pushing, the great old root was safe on the hearth and beginning to crackle and blaze with the red embers. In high glee, the cobblers sat down to their beer and bacon. The door was shut, for there was nothing but cold moonlight and snow outside; but the hut, strewn with fir boughs, and ornamented with holly, looked cheerful as the ruddy blaze flared up and rejoiced their hearts.

'Long life and good fortune to ourselves, brother!' said Spare. 'I hope you will drink that toast, and may we never have a worse fire on Christmas – but what is that?'

Spare set down the drinking-horn, and the brothers listened astonished, for out of the blazing root they heard, 'Cuckoo! cuckoo!' as plain as ever the spring-bird's voice came over the moor on a May morning.

'It is something bad,' said Scrub, terribly frightened.

'Maybe not,' said Spare; and out of the deep hole at the side which the fire had not reached flew a large grey cuckoo, and lit on the table before them. Much as the cobblers had been surprised, they were still more so when it said:

'Good gentlemen, what season is this?'

'It's Christmas,' said Spare.

'Then a merry Christmas to you!' said the cuckoo. 'I went to sleep in the hollow of that old root one evening last summer and never woke till the heat of your fire made me think it was summer again; but now, since you have burned my lodging, let me stay in your hut till the spring comes round – I only want a hole to sleep in, and when I go on my travels next summer be assured I will bring you some present for your trouble.'

'Stay, and welcome,' said Spare, while Scrub sat wondering if it were something bad or not; 'I'll make you a good warm hole in the thatch. But you must be hungry after that long sleep. Here is a slice of barley bread. Come, help us to keep Christmas!'

The cuckoo ate up the slice, drank water from the brown jug, for he would take no beer, and flew into a snug hole which Spare scooped for him in the thatch of the hut.

Scrub said he was afraid it wouldn't be lucky; but as it slept on and the days passed he forgot his fears. So the snow melted, the heavy rains came, the cold grew less, the days lengthened, and one sunny morning the brothers were awakened by the cuckoo shouting its own cry to let them know the spring had come.

'Now I'm going on my travels,' said the bird, 'over the world to tell men of the spring. There is no country where trees bud or flowers bloom that I will not cry in before the year goes round. Give me another slice of barley bread to keep me on my journey and tell me what present I shall bring you at the twelvemonth's end.'

Scrub would have been angry with his brother for cutting so large a slice, their store of barley-meal being low; but his mind was occupied with what present would be most prudent to ask: at length a lucky thought struck him.

'Good master cuckoo,' said he, 'if a great traveller who sees all the world

like you, could know of any place where diamonds or pearls were to be found, one of a tolerable size brought in your beak would help such poor men as my brother and I to provide something better than barley bread for your next entertainment.'

'I know nothing of diamonds or pearls,' said the cuckoo; 'they are in the hearts of rocks and the sands of rivers. My knowledge is only of that which grows on the earth. But there are two trees hard by the well that lies at the world's end: one of them is called the golden tree, for its leaves are all of beaten gold; every winter they fall into the well with a sound like scattered coins, and I know not what becomes of them. As for the other, it is always green like a laurel. Some call it the wise, and some the merry tree. Its leaves never fall, but they that get one of them keep a blithe heart in spite of all misfortunes and can make themselves as merry in a hut as in a palace.'

'Good master cuckoo, bring me a leaf off that tree!' cried Spare.

'Now, brother, don't be a fool!' said Scrub. 'Think of the leaves of beaten gold! Dear master cuckoo, bring me one of them!'

Before another word could be spoken, the cuckoo had flown out of the open door, and was shouting its spring cry over moor and meadow. The brothers were poorer than ever that year; nobody would send them a single shoe to mend. The new cobbler said in scorn they should come to be his apprentices; and Scrub and Spare would have left the village but for their barley-field, their cabbage garden and a certain maid called Fairfeather, whom both the cobblers had courted for seven years without even knowing which she meant to favour.

Sometimes Fairfeather seemed inclined to Scrub, sometimes she smiled on Spare; but the brothers never disputed for that. They sowed their barley, planted their cabbage and, now that their trade was gone, worked in the rich villagers' fields to make out a scanty living. So the seasons came and passed: spring, summer, harvest and winter followed each other as they have done from the beginning. At the end of the last, Scrub and Spare had grown so poor and ragged that Fairfeather thought them beneath her notice. Old neighbours forgot to invite them to wedding feasts or merrymaking; and they thought the cuckoo had forgotten them too, when at daybreak, on the first of April, they heard a hard beak knocking at their door and a voice crying:

'Cuckoo! cuckoo! Let me in with my presents.'

Spare ran to open the door, and in came the cuckoo, carrying on one side of his bill a golden leaf larger than that of any tree in the north country; and in the other, one like that of the common laurel, only it had a fresher green.

'Here,' it said, giving the gold to Scrub and the green to Spare, 'it is a long carriage from the world's end. Give me a slice of barley bread, for I must tell the north country that the spring has come.'

Scrub did not grudge the thickness of that slice, though it was cut from their last loaf. So much gold had never been in the cobbler's hands before and he could not help exulting over his brother.

'See the wisdom of my choice!' he said, holding up the large leaf of gold. 'As for yours, as good might be plucked from any hedge. I wonder a sensible bird would carry the like so far.'

'Good master cobbler,' cried the cuckoo, finishing the slice, 'your conclusions are more hasty than courteous. If your brother be disappointed this time, I go on the same journey every year, and for your hospitable entertainment will think it no trouble to bring each of you whichever leaf you desire.'

'Darling cuckoo,' cried Scrub, 'bring me a golden one'; and Spare, looking up from the green leaf on which he gazed as though it were a crown jewel, said:

'Be sure to bring me one from the merry tree,' and away flew the cuckoo.

'This is the Feast of All Fools, and it ought to be your birthday,' said Scrub. 'Did ever man fling away such an opportunity of getting rich! Much good your merry leaves will do in the midst of rags and poverty!' So he went on, but Spare laughed at him and answered with quaint old proverbs concerning the cares that come with gold, till Scrub, at length getting angry, vowed his brother was not fit to live with a respectable man; and taking his lasts, his awls and his golden leaf, he left the wattle hut and went to tell the villagers.

They were astonished at the folly of Spare and charmed with Scrub's good sense, particularly when he showed them the golden leaf, and told that the cuckoo would bring him one every spring. The new cobbler immediately took him into partnership, the greatest people sent him their shoes to mend, Fairfeather smiled graciously upon him and in the course of that summer they were married, with a grand wedding feast, at which the whole village danced, except Spare, who was not invited, because the bride could not bear his low-mindedness, and his brother thought him a disgrace to the family.

Indeed all who heard the story concluded that Spare must be mad, and nobody would associate with him but a lame tinker, a beggar-boy and a poor woman reputed to be a witch because she was old and ugly. As for Scrub, he established himself with Fairfeather in a cottage close by that of the new cobbler, and quite as fine. There he mended shoes to everybody's satisfaction, had a scarlet coat for holidays and a fat goose for dinner every wedding-day. Fairfeather, too, had a crimson gown and fine blue ribands; but neither she nor Scrub were content, for to buy this grandeur the golden leaf had to be broken and parted with piece by piece, so the last morsel was gone before the cuckoo came with another.

Spare lived on in the old hut, and worked in the cabbage garden. (Scrub had got the barley-field because he was the elder.) Every day his coat grew more ragged, and the hut more weatherbeaten; but people remarked that he never looked sad nor sour; and the wonder was that, from the time they began to keep his company, the tinker grew kinder to the poor ass with which he travelled the country, the beggar-boy kept out of mischief and the old woman was never cross to her cat or angry with the children.

Every first of April the cuckoo came tapping at their doors with the golden leaf to Scrub and the green to Spare. Fairfeather would have entertained him nobly with wheaten bread and honey, for she had some notion of persuading him to bring two gold leaves instead of one; but the cuckoo flew away to eat barley bread with Spare, saying he was not fit company for fine people, and liked the old hut where he slept so snugly from Christmas till spring.

Scrub spent the golden leaves, and Spare kept the merry ones; and I know not how many years passed in this manner, when a certain great lord who owned that village came to the neighbourhood. His castle stood on the moor: It was ancient and strong, with high towers and a deep moat. All the country, as far as one could see from the highest turret,

belonged to its lord; but he had not been there for twenty years, and would not have come then, only he was melancholy. The cause of his grief was that he had been prime minister at court and in high favour, till somebody told the crown prince that he had spoken disrespectfully concerning the turning out of his royal highness's toes, and of the king that he did not lay on taxes enough, whereon the north country lord was turned out of office and banished to his own estate. There he lived for some weeks in very bad temper. The servants said nothing would please him, and the villagers put on their worst clothes lest he should raise their rents; but one day in the harvest time his lordship chanced to meet Spare gathering watercresses at a meadow stream, and fell into talk with the cobbler.

How it was nobody could tell, but from the hour of that discourse the great lord cast away his melancholy: he forgot his lost office and his court enemies, the king's taxes and the crown prince's toes, and went about with a noble train, hunting, fishing and making merry in his hall, where all travellers were entertained and all the poor were welcome. This strange story spread through the north country, and great company came to the cobbler's hut – rich men who had lost their money, poor men who had lost their friends, beauties who had grown old, wits who had gone out of fashion – all came to talk with Spare, and whatever their troubles had been, all went home merry. The rich gave him presents, the poor gave him thanks. Spare's coat ceased to be ragged, he had bacon with his cabbage and the villagers began to think there was some sense in him.

By this time his fame had reached the capital city, and even the court. There were a great many discontented people there besides the king, who had lately fallen into ill humour because a neighbouring princess, with seven islands for her dowry, would not marry his eldest son. So a royal messenger was sent to Spare, with a velvet mantle, a diamond ring and a command that he should repair to court immediately.

'Tomorrow is the first of April,' said Spare, 'and I will go with you two hours after sunrise.'

The messenger lodged all night at the castle, and the cuckoo came at sunrise with the merry leaf.

'Court is a fine place,' he said when the cobbler told him he was going, 'but I cannot come there, they would lay snares and catch me; so be careful of the leaves I have brought you, and give me a farewell slice of barley bread.'

Spare was sorry to part with the cuckoo, little as he had of his company; but he gave him a slice which would have broken Scrub's heart in former times, it was so thick and large; and having sewed up the leaves in the lining of his leather doublet, he set out with the messenger on his way to court.

His coming caused great surprise there. Everybody wondered what the king could see in such a common-looking man; but scarce had his majesty conversed with him half an hour, when the princess and her seven islands were forgotten, and orders given that a feast for all comers should be spread in the banquet hall. The princes of the blood, the great lords and ladies, ministers of state and judges of the land, after that, discoursed with Spare, and the more they talked the lighter grew their hearts, so that such changes had never been seen at court. The lords forgot their spites and the ladies their envies, the princes and ministers made friends among themselves, and the judges showed no favour.

As for Spare, he had a chamber assigned him in the palace and a seat at the king's table; one sent him rich robes and another costly jewels; but in the midst of all his grandeur he still wore the leathern doublet, which the palace servants thought remarkably mean. One day the king's attention being drawn to it by the chief page, his majesty inquired why Spare didn't give it to a beggar? But the cobbler answered:

'High and mighty monarch, this doublet was with me before silk and velvet came – I find it easier to wear than the court cut; moreover it serves to keep me humble, by recalling the days when it was my holiday garment.'

The king thought this a wise speech, and commanded that no one should find fault with the leathern doublet. So things went, till tidings of his brother's good fortune reached Scrub in the moorland cottage on another first of April, when the cuckoo came with two golden leaves, because he had none to carry for Spare.

'Think of that!' said Fairfeather. 'Here we are spending our lives in this humdrum place, and Spare making his fortune at court with two or three paltry green leaves! What would they say to our golden ones? Let us pack up and make our way to the king's palace; I'm sure he will make you a lord and me a lady of honour, not to speak of all the fine clothes and presents we shall have.'

Scrub thought this excellent reasoning, and their packing up began; but it was soon found that the cottage contained few things fit for carrying to court. Fairfeather could not think of her wooden bowls, spoons and trenchers being seen there. Scrub considered his lasts and awls better left behind, as without them, he concluded, no one would suspect him of being a cobbler. So putting on their holiday clothes, Fairfeather took her looking-glass and Scrub his drinking-horn, which happened to have a very thin rim of silver, and each carrying a golden leaf carefully wrapped up that none might see it till they reached the palace, the pair set out in great expectation.

How far Scrub and Fairfeather journeyed I cannot say, but when the sun was high and warm at noon, they came into a wood both tired and hungry.

'If I had known it was so far to court,' said Scrub, I would have brought the end of that barley loaf which we left in the cupboard.'

'Husband,' said Fairfeather, 'you shouldn't have such mean thoughts: how could one eat barley bread on the way to a palace? Let us rest ourselves under this tree, and look at our golden leaves to see if they are safe.' In looking at the leaves, and talking of their fine prospects, Scrub and Fairfeather did not perceive that a very thin old woman had slipped from behind the tree, with a long staff in her hand and a great wallet by her side.

'Noble lord and lady,' she said, 'for I know you are such by your voices, though my eyes are dim and my hearing none of the sharpest, will you condescend to tell me where I may find some water to mix a bottle of mead which I carry in my wallet, because it is too strong for me?'

As the old woman spoke, she pulled out a large wooden bottle such as shepherds used in the ancient times, corked with leaves rolled together and having a small wooden cup hanging from its handle.

'Perhaps you will do me the favour to taste,' she said. 'It is only made of the best honey. I have also cream cheese and a wheaten loaf here, if such honourable persons as you would eat the like.'

Scrub and Fairfeather became very condescending after this speech. They were now sure that there must be some appearance of nobility about them; besides, they were very hungry, and having hastily wrapped up the golden leaves, they assured the old woman they were not at all proud, notwithstanding the lands and castles they had left behind them in the north country, and would willingly help to lighten the wallet. The old woman could scarcely be persuaded to sit down for pure humility, but at length she did, and before the wallet was half empty Scrub and

Fairfeather firmly believed that there must be something remarkably noble-looking about them. This was not entirely owing to her ingenious discourse. The old woman was a wood-witch; her name was Buttertongue; and all her time was spent in making mead, which, being boiled with curious herbs and spells, had the power of making all who drank it fall asleep and dream with their eyes open. She had two dwarfs of sons; one was named Spy and the other Pounce. Wherever their

mother went they were not far behind; and whoever tasted her mead was sure to be robbed by the dwarfs.

Scrub and Fairfeather sat leaning against the old tree. The cobbler had a lump of cheese in his hand; his wife held fast a hunch of bread. Their eyes and mouths were both open, but they were dreaming of great grandeur at court, when the old woman raised her shrill voice:

'What ho, my sons, come here and carry home the harvest!'

No sooner had she spoken than the two little dwarfs darted out of the neighbouring thicket.

'Idle boys!' cried the mother. 'What have you done today to help our living?'

'I have been to the city,' said Spy, 'and could see nothing. These are hard times for us – everybody minds his business so contentedly since that cobbler came; but here is a leathern doublet which his page threw out of the window; it's of no use, but I brought it to let you see I was not idle.' And he tossed down Spare's doublet, with the merry leaves in it, which he had carried like a bundle on his little back.

To explain how Spy came by it, I must tell you that the forest was not far from the great city where Spare lived in such high esteem. All things had gone well with the cobbler till the king thought it was quite unbecoming to see such a worthy man without a servant. His majesty, therefore, to let all men understand his royal favour towards Spare, appointed one of his own pages to wait upon him. The name of this youth was Tinseltoes, and though he was the seventh of the king's pages nobody in all the court had grander notions. Nothing could please him that had not gold or silver about it, and his grandmother feared he would hang himself for being appointed page to a cobbler. As for Spare, if anything could have troubled him, this token of his majesty's kindness would have done it.

The honest man had been so used to serve himself that the page was always in the way, but his merry leaves came to his assistance; and, to the great surprise of his grandmother, Tinseltoes took wonderfully to the new service. Some said it was because Spare gave him nothing to do but play at bowls all day on the palace green. Yet one thing grieved the heart of Tinseltoes, and that was his master's leathern doublet; but for it, he was persuaded, people would never remember that Spare had been a cobbler, and the page took a deal of pains to let him see how unfashionable it was at court; but Spare answered Tinseltoes as he had done the king, and at last, finding nothing better would do, the page got up one fine morning earlier than his master, and tossed the leathern doublet out of the back window into a certain lane where Spy found it, and brought it to his mother.

'That nasty thing!' said the old woman. 'Where is the good in it?'

By this time Pounce had taken everything of value from Scrub and Fairfeather – the looking-glass, the silver-rimmed horn, the husband's scarlet coat, the wife's gay mantle, and above all the golden leaves, which so rejoiced old Buttertongue and her sons that they threw the leathern doublet over the sleeping cobbler for a jest, and went off to their hut in the heart of the forest.

The sun was going down when Scrub and Fairfeather awoke from dreaming that they had been made a lord and a lady and sat clothed in silk and velvet, feasting with the king in his palace hall. It was a great disappointment to find their golden leaves and all their best things gone. Scrub tore his hair and vowed to take the old woman's life, while Fairfeather lamented sore; but Scrub, feeling cold for want of his coat, put on the leathern doublet without asking or caring whence it came.

Scarcely was it buttoned on when a change came over him; he addressed such merry discourse to Fairfeather, that, instead of lamentations, she made the wood ring with laughter. Both busied themselves in getting up a hut of boughs in which Scrub kindled a fire with a flint and steel, which, together with his pipe, he had brought unknown to Fairfeather, who had told him the like was never heard of at court. Then they found a pheasant's nest at the root of an old oak, made a meal of roasted eggs, and went to sleep on a heap of long green grass which they had gathered, with nightingales singing all night long in the old trees about them. So it happened that Scrub and Fairfeather stayed day after day in the forest, making their hut larger and more comfortable against the winter, living on wild birds' eggs and berries and never thinking of their lost golden leaves, or their journey to court.

In the meantime Spare had got up and missed his doublet. Tinseltoes, of course, said he knew nothing about it. The whole palace was searched, and every servant questioned, till all the court wondered why such a fuss was made about an old leathern doublet. That very day things came back to their old fashion. Quarrels began among the lords and jealousies among the ladies. The king said his subjects did not pay him half enough taxes, the queen wanted more jewels, the servants took to their old bickerings and got up some new ones. Spare found himself getting wonderfully dull, and very much out of place: nobles began to ask what business a cobbler had at the king's table, and his majesty ordered the palace chronicles to be searched for a precedent. The cobbler was too wise to tell all he had lost with that doublet, but being by this time somewhat familiar with court customs, he proclaimed a reward of fifty gold pieces to any who would bring him news concerning it.

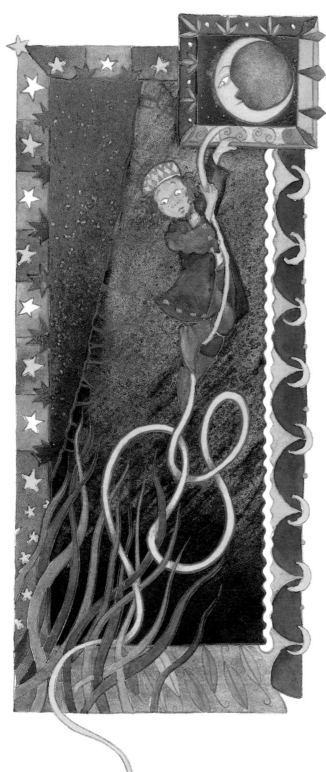

Scarcely was this made known in the city when the gates and outer courts of the palace were filled by men, women and children, some bringing leathern doublets of every cut and colour – some with tales of what they had heard and seen in their walks about the neighbourhood. And so much news concerning all sorts of great people came out of these stories that lords and ladies ran to the king with complaints of Spare as a speaker of slander; and his majesty, being now satisfied that there was no example in all the palace records of such a retainer, issued a decree banishing the cobbler for ever from court and confiscating all his goods in favour of Tinseltoes.

That royal edict was scarcely published before the page was in full possession of his rich chamber, his costly garments and all the presents the courtiers had given him; while Spare, having no longer the fifty pieces of gold to give, was glad to make his escape out of the back window, for fear of the nobles, who vowed to be revenged on him, and the crowd, who were prepared to stone him for cheating them about his doublet.

The window from which Spare let himself down with a strong rope was that from which Tinseltoes had tossed the doublet, and as the cobbler came down late in the twilight, a poor woodman with a heavy load of faggots stopped and stared at him in great astonishment.

'What's the matter, friend?' said Spare. 'Did you never see a man coming down from a back window before?'

'Why,' said the woodman, 'the last morning I passed here a leathern doublet came out of that very window, and I'll be bound you are the owner of it.'

'That I am, friend,' said the cobbler. 'Can you tell me which way that doublet went?'

'As I walked on,' said the woodman, 'a dwarf, called Spy, bundled it up and ran off to his mother in the forest.'

'Honest friend,' said Spare, taking off the last of his fine clothes (a grass-green mantle edged with gold), 'I'll give you this if you will follow the dwarf and bring me back my doublet.'

'It would not be good to carry faggots in,' said the woodman. 'But if you want back your doublet, the road to the forest lies at the end of this lane,' and he trudged away.

Determined to find his doublet, and sure that neither crowd nor courtiers could catch him in the forest, Spare went on his way, and was soon among the tall trees; but neither hut nor dwarf could he see. Moreover the night came on; the wood was dark and tangled, but here and there the moon shone through its alleys, the great owls flitted about, and the nightingales sang. So he went on, hoping to find some place of shelter. At last the red light of a fire, gleaming through a thicket, led him to the door of a low hut. It stood half open, as if there was nothing to fear, and within he saw his brother Scrub snoring loudly on a bed of grass, at the foot of which lay his own leathern doublet; while Fairfeather, in a kirtle made of plaited rushes, sat roasting pheasants' eggs by the fire.

'Good evening, mistress,' said Spare, stepping in.

The blaze shone on him, but so changed was her brother-in-law with his court life, that Fairfeather did not know him, and she answered far more courteously than was her wont.

'Good evening, master. Whence come ye so late? But speak low, for my good man has sorely tired himself cleaving wood, and is taking a sleep, as you see, before supper.'

'A good rest to him,' said Spare, perceiving he was not known. 'I come from the court for a day's hunting, and have lost my way in the forest.'

'Sit down and have a share of our supper,' said Fairfeather. 'I will put some more eggs in the ashes; and tell me the news of court – I used to think of it long ago when I was young and foolish.'

'Did you never go there?' said the cobbler. 'So fair a dame as you would make the ladies marvel.'

'You are pleased to flatter,' said Fairfeather; 'but my husband has a brother there, and we left our moorland village to try our fortune also. An old woman enticed us with fair words and strong drink at the entrance of the forest, where we fell asleep and dreamt of great things; but when we woke, everything had been robbed from us – my looking-glass, my scarlet cloak, my husband's Sunday coat; and, in place of all, the robbers left him that old leathern doublet, which he has worn ever since, and never was so merry in all his life, though we live in this poor hut.'

'It is a shabby doublet, that,' said Spare, taking up the garment, and seeing that it was his own, for the merry leaves were still sewed in its lining. 'It would be good for hunting in, however – your husband would be glad to part with it, I dare say, in exchange for this handsome cloak;' and he pulled off the green mantle and buttoned on the doublet, much to Fairfeather's delight, who ran and shook Scrub, crying:

'Husband! husband! rise and see what a good bargain I have made!'

Scrub gave one closing snore, and muttered something about the root being hard; but he rubbed his eyes, gazed up at his brother, and said:

'Spare, is that really you? How did you like the court, and have you made your fortune?'

'That I have, brother,' said Spare, 'in getting back my own good leathern doublet. Come, let us eat eggs and rest ourselves here this night. In the morning we will return to our own old hut, at the end of the moorland village where the Christmas Cuckoo will come and bring us leaves.'

Scrub and Fairfeather agreed. So in the morning they all returned, and found the old hut the worse for wear and weather. The neighbours came about them to ask the news of court, and see if they had made their fortune. Everybody was astonished to find the three poorer than ever, but somehow they liked to go back to the hut. Spare brought out the lasts and awls he had hidden in a corner; Scrub and he began their old trade, and the whole north country found out that there never were such cobblers.

They mended the shoes of lords and ladies as well as the common people; everybody was satisfied. Their custom increased from day to day, and all that were disappointed, discontented or unlucky came to the hut as in old times before Spare went to court.

The rich brought them presents, the poor did them service. The hut itself changed, no one knew how. Flowering honeysuckle grew over its roof; red and white roses grew thick about its door. Moreover the Christmas Cuckoo always came on the first of April, bringing three leaves of the merry tree – for Scrub and Fairfeather would have no more golden ones. So it was with them when I last heard the news of the north country.

'What a summer-house that hut would make for me, mamma!' said the Princess Greedalind.

'We must have it brought here bodily,' said Queen Wantall; but the chair was silent, and a lady and two noble squires, clad in russet-coloured satin and yellow buskins, the like of which had never been seen at that court, rose up and said:

'That's our story.'

'I have not heard such a tale,' said King Winwealth, 'since my brother Wisewit went from me and was lost in the forest. Redheels, the seventh of my pages, go and bring this little maid a pair of scarlet shoes with golden buckles.'

The seventh page immediately brought from the royal store a pair of scarlet satin shoes with buckles of gold. Snowflower never had seen the like before, and joyfully thanking the king, she dropped a curtsy, seated herself and said: 'Chair of my grandmother, take me to the worst kitchen.' Immediately the chair marched away as it came, to the admiration of that noble company.

The little girl was allowed to sleep on some straw at the kitchen fire that night. Next day they gave her ale with the scraps the cook threw away. The feast went on with great music and splendour, and without the people clamoured; but in the evening King Winwealth again fell into low spirits, and the royal command was told to Snowflower by the chief scullion, that she and her chair should go to the highest banquet hall, for his majesty wished to hear another story.

When Snowflower had washed her face and dusted her chair, she went

up seated as before, only that she had on the scarlet shoes. Queen Wantall and her daughter looked more spiteful than ever, but some of the company graciously noticed Snowflower's curtsy, and were pleased when she laid down her head, saying: 'Chair of my grandmother, tell me a story.'

'Listen,' said the clear voice from under the cushion, 'to the story of Lady Greensleeves.'

Chapter 3

The Lords
of the
White and Grey Castles

Once upon a time there lived two noble lords in the east country. Their lands lay between a broad river and an old oak forest, whose size was so great that no man knew it. In the midst of his land each lord had a stately castle; one was built of the white freestone, the other of the grey granite. So the one was called Lord of the White Castle, and the other Lord of the Grey.

There were no lords like them in all the east country for nobleness and bounty. Their tenants lived in peace and plenty; all strangers were hospitably entertained at their castle; and every autumn they sent men with axes into the forest to hew down the great trees and chop them up into firewood for the poor. Neither hedge nor ditch divided their lands, but these lords never disputed. They had been friends from their youth. Their ladies had died long ago, but the Lord of the Grey Castle had a little son, and the Lord of the White a little daughter; and when they feasted in each other's halls it was their custom to say: 'When our children grow up they will marry, and have our castles and our lands, and keep our friendship in memory.'

So the lords and their little children, and tenants, lived happily till one Michaelmas night, as they were all feasting in the hall of the White Castle, there came a traveller to the gate, who was welcomed and feasted as usual. He had seen many strange sights and countries, and, like most people, he liked to tell of his travels. The lords were delighted with his tales, as they sat round the fire drinking wine after supper, and at length the Lord of the White Castle, who was very curious, said:

'Good stranger, what was the greatest wonder you ever saw in all your travels?'

'The most wonderful sight that ever I saw,' replied the traveller, 'was at the end of yonder forest, where in an ancient wooden house there sits an old woman weaving her own hair into grey cloth on an old crazy loom. When she wants more yarn she cuts off her own grey hair, and it grows so quickly that though I saw it cut in the morning, it was out of the door before noon. She told me it was her purpose to sell the cloth, but none of all who came that way had yet bought any, she asked so great a price; and, only the way is so long and dangerous through that wide forest full of boars and wolves, some rich lord like you might buy it for a mantle.'

All who heard this story were astonished; but when the traveller had gone on his way the Lord of the White Castle could neither eat nor sleep for wishing to see the old woman that wove her own hair. At length he made up his mind to explore the forest in search of her ancient house, and told the Lord of the Grey Castle his intention. Being a prudent man, this lord replied that travellers' tales were not always to be trusted and earnestly advised him against undertaking such a long and dangerous journey, for few that went far into that forest ever returned. However, when the curious lord would go in spite of all, he vowed to bear him company for friendship's sake, and they agreed to set out privately, lest the other lords of the land might laugh at them. The Lord of the White Castle had a steward who had served him many years, and his name was Reckoning Robin. To him he said:

'I am going on a long journey with my friend. Be careful of my goods, deal justly with my tenants, and above all things be kind to my little daughter Loveleaves till my return;' and the steward answered:

'Be sure, my lord, I will.'

The Lord of the Grey Castle also had a steward who had served him many years, and his name was Wary Will. To him he said:

'I am going on a journey with my friend. Be careful of my goods, deal justly with my tenants, and above all things be kind to my little son Woodwender till my return;' and his steward answered him:

'Be sure, my lord, I will.'

So these lords kissed their children while they slept, and set out each with his staff and mantle before sunrise through the old oak forest. The children missed their fathers; the tenants missed their lords. None but the stewards could tell what had become of them; but seven months wore away, and they did not come back. The lords had thought their stewards faithful, because they served so well under their eyes; but instead of that, both were proud and crafty, and thinking that some evil had happened to their masters, they set themselves to be lords in their place.

Reckoning Robin had a son called Hardhold, and Wary Will a daughter called Drypenny. There was not a sulkier boy or girl in the country, but their fathers resolved to make a young lord and lady of them; so they took the silk clothes which Woodwender and Loveleaves used to wear to dress them, clothing the lords' children in frieze and canvas. Their garden flowers and ivory toys were given to Hardhold and Drypenny; and at last the stewards' children sat at the chief tables and slept in the best chambers, while Woodwender and Loveleaves were sent to herd the swine and sleep on straw in the granary.

The poor children had no one to take their part. Every morning at sunrise they were sent out – each with a barley loaf and a bottle of sour milk, which was to serve them for breakfast, dinner and supper – to watch a great herd of swine on a wide, unfenced pasture hard by the forest. The grass was scanty, and the swine were continually straying into the wood in search of acorns; the children knew that if they were lost the wicked stewards would punish them; and between gathering and keeping their herds in order, they were readier to sleep on the granary straw at night than ever they had been within their own silken curtains. Still, Woodwender and Loveleaves helped and comforted each other, saying their fathers would come back, or God would send them some friends: so, in spite of swine-herding and hard living, they looked blithe and handsome as ever; while Hardhold and Drypenny grew crosser and uglier every day, notwithstanding their fine clothes and the best of all things.

The crafty stewards did not like this. They thought their children ought to look genteel, and Woodwender and Loveleaves like young swineherds; so they sent them to a wilder pasture, still nearer the forest, and gave them two great black hogs, more unruly than all the rest to keep. One of these hogs belonged to Hardhold, and the other to Drypenny. Every evening when they came home the stewards' children used to come down and feed them, and it was their delight to reckon up what price they would bring when properly fattened.

One sultry day, about midsummer, Woodwender and Loveleaves sat down in the shadow of a mossy rock: the swine grazed about them more quietly than usual, and they plaited rushes and talked to each other, till, as the sun was sloping down the sky, Woodwender saw that the two great hogs were missing. Thinking they must have gone to the forest, the poor children ran to search for them. They heard the thrush singing and the wood-doves calling; they saw the squirrels leaping from bough to bough and the great deer bounding by; but though they searched for hours, no trace of the favourite hogs could be seen. Loveleaves and Woodwender durst not go home without them. Deeper and deeper they ran into the forest, searching and calling, but all in vain; and when the woods began to darken with the fall of evening, the children feared they had lost their way.

It was known that they never feared the forest, nor all the boars and wolves that were in it; but being weary, they wished for some place of shelter and took a green path through the trees, thinking it might lead to the dwelling of some hermit or forester. A fairer way Woodwender and Loveleaves had never walked. The grass was soft and mossy, a hedge of wild roses and honeysuckle grew on either side and the red light of sunset streamed through the tall trees above. On they went, and it led them straight to a great open dell, covered with the loveliest flowers, bordered with banks of wild strawberries, and all overshadowed by one enormous oak, whose like had never been seen in grove or forest. Its branches were as large as full-grown trees. Its trunk was wider than a country church and its height like that of a castle. There were mossy seats at its great root, and when the tired children had gathered as many strawberries as they cared for they sat down on one, hard by a small spring that bubbled up as clear as crystal. The huge oak was covered with thick ivy, in which thousands of birds had their nests. Woodwender and Loveleaves watched them

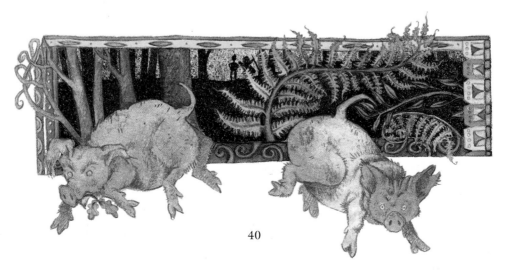

flying home from all parts
of the forest, and at last they
saw a lady coming by the same path
which led them to the dell. She wore a
gown of russet colour; her yellow hair was
braided and bound with a crimson fillet. In her right
hand she carried a holly branch; but the most
remarkable part of her attire was a pair of long sleeves,
as green as the very grass.

'Who are you?' she said, 'that sit so late beside my
well?' and the children told her their story, how
they had first lost the hogs, then their way, and were
afraid to go home to the wicked stewards.

'Well,' said the lady, 'ye are the fairest
swineherds that ever came this way. Choose
whether ye will go home and keep hogs for
Hardhold and Drypenny, or live in the free
forest with me.'

'We will stay with you,' said the children, 'for we like not keeping swine. Besides, our fathers went through this forest, and we may meet them some day coming home.'

While they spoke the lady slipped her holly branch through the ivy, as if it had been a key; presently a door opened in the oak, and there was a fair house. The windows were of rock crystal, but they could not be seen from without. The walls and floor were covered with thick green moss, as soft as velvet. There were low seats and a round table, vessels of carved wood, a hearth inlaid with curious stones, an oven and a store chamber for provisions against the winter. When they stepped in the lady said:

'A hundred years have I lived here, and my name is Lady Greensleeves. No friend or servant have I had except my dwarf, Corner, who comes to me at the end of harvest with his handmill, his pannier and his axe: with these he grinds the nuts and gathers the berries and cleaves the firewood, and blithely we live all the winter. But Corner loves the frost and fears the sun, and when the topmost boughs begin to bud, he returns to his country far in the north, so I am lonely in the summer time.'

By this discourse the children saw how welcome they were. Lady Greensleeves gave them does' milk and cakes of nut-flour, and soft green moss to sleep on; and they forgot all their troubles, the wicked stewards and the straying swine. Early in the morning a troop of does came to be milked, fairies brought flowers and birds brought berries, to show Lady Greensleeves what had bloomed and ripened. She taught the children to make cheese of the does' milk, and wine of the woodberries. She showed them the stores of honey which wild bees had made and left in hollow trees, the rarest plants of the forest and the herbs that made all its creatures tame.

All that summer Woodwender and Loveleaves lived with her in the great oak tree, free from toil and care; and the children would have been happy, but they could hear no tidings of their fathers. At last the leaves began to fade, and the flowers to fall; Lady Greensleeves said that Corner was coming; and one moonlight night she heaped sticks on the fire and set her door open, when Woodwender and Loveleaves were going to sleep, saying she expected some old friends to tell her the news of the forest.

Loveleaves was not quite so curious as her father, the Lord of the White Castle, but she kept awake to see what would happen, and terribly frightened the little girl was when in walked a great brown bear.

'Good evening, lady,' said the bear.

'Good evening, bear,' said Lady Greensleeves. 'What is the news in your neighbourhood?'

'Not much,' said the bear; 'only the fawns are growing very cunning – one can't catch above three in a day.'

'That's bad news,' said Lady Greensleeves; and immediately in walked a great wild cat.

'Good evening, lady,' said the cat.

'Good evening, cat,' said Lady Greensleeves. 'What is the news in your neighbourhood?'

'Not much,' said the cat; 'only the birds are growing very plentiful – it is not worth one's while to catch them.'

'That's good news,' said Lady Greensleeves; and in flew a great black raven.

'Good evening, lady,' said the raven.

'Good evening, raven,' said Lady Greensleeves. 'What is the news in your neighbourhood?'

'Not much,' said the raven; 'only in a hundred years or so we shall be very genteel and private – the trees will be so thick.'

'How is that?' said Lady Greensleeves.

'Oh,' said the raven, 'have you not heard how the king of the forest fairies laid a spell on two noble lords, who were travelling through his dominions to see the old woman that weaves her own hair? They had thinned his oaks every year, cutting firewood for the poor: so the king met them in the likeness of a hunter, and asked them to drink out of his oaken goblet, because the day was warm. And when the two lords drank, they forgot their lands and their tenants, their castles and their children, and minded nothing in all this world but the planting of acorns, which they do day and night by the power of the spell in the heart of the forest, and will never cease till someone makes them pause in their work before the sun sets, and then the spell will be broken.'

'Ah,' said Lady Greensleeves, 'he is a great prince, that king of the forest fairies; and there is worse work in the world than planting acorns.'

Soon after, the bear, the cat and the raven bade Greensleeves goodnight. She closed the door, put out the light and went to sleep on the soft moss as usual.

In the morning Loveleaves told Woodwender what she had heard, and they went to Lady Greensleeves where she milked the does and said:

'We heard what the raven told last night, and we know the two lords are our fathers: tell us how the spell may be broken!'

'I fear the king of the forest fairies,' said Lady Greensleeves, 'because I live here alone, and have no friend but my dwarf Corner; but I will tell you what you may do. At the end of the path which leads from this dell turn your faces to the north, and you will find a narrow way sprinkled over with black feathers. Keep that path, no matter how it winds, and it will lead you straight to the ravens' neighbourhood, where you will find your fathers planting acorns under the forest trees. Watch till the sun is near setting, and tell them the most wonderful things you know to make them forget their work; but be sure to tell nothing but truth, and drink nothing but running water, or you will fall into the power of the fairy king.'

The children thanked her for this good counsel. She packed up cakes and cheese for them in a bag of woven grass, and they soon found the narrow way sprinkled over with black feathers. It was very long, and wound through the thick trees in so many circles that the children were often weary and sat down to rest. When the night came they found a mossy hollow in the trunk of an old tree, where they laid themselves down and slept all the summer night – for Woodwender and Loveleaves never feared the forest. So they went, eating their cakes and cheese when they were hungry, drinking from the running stream and sleeping in the hollow trees, till on the evening of the seventh day they came into the ravens' neighbourhood. The tall trees were laden with nests and black with ravens. There was nothing to be heard but continual cawing; and in a great opening where the oaks grew thinnest, the children saw their own fathers busy planting acorns. Each lord had on the velvet mantle in which he left his castle, but it was worn to rags with rough work in the forest. Their hair and beards had grown long; their hands were soiled with earth; each had an old wooden spade, and on all sides lay heaps of acorns. The children called them by their names, and ran to kiss them, each saying: 'Dear father, come back to your castle and your people!' but the lords replied:

'We know of no castles and no people. There is nothing in all this world but oak trees and acorns.'

Woodwender and Loveleaves told them of all their former state in vain – nothing would make them pause for a minute: so the poor children first sat down and cried, and then slept on the cold grass, for the sun set, and the lords worked on. When they awoke it was broad day; Woodwender cheered up his sister, saying: 'We are hungry, and there are still two cakes in the bag; let us share one of them – who knows but something may happen?'

So they divided the cake and ran to the lords, saying: 'Dear fathers, eat with us;' but the lords said:

'There is no use for meat or drink. Let us plant our acorns.

Loveleaves and Woodwender sat down and ate their cake in great sorrow. When they had finished, both went to a stream hard by and began to drink the clear water with a large acorn shell; and as they drank there came through the oaks a gay young hunter whose mantle was green as the grass, about his neck there hung a crystal bugle, and in his hand he carried a huge oaken goblet, carved with flowers and leaves, and rimmed with crystal. Up to the brim it was filled with milk, on which the rich cream floated; and as the hunter came near he said, 'Fair children, leave that muddy water and come and drink with me;' but Woodwender and Loveleaves answered:

'Thanks, good hunter, but we have promised to drink nothing but running water.' Still the hunter came nearer with his goblet, saying:

'The water is foul: it may do for swineherds and woodcutters, but not for such fair children as you. Tell me, are you not the children of mighty kings? Were you not reared in palaces?' But the boy and girl answered him:

'No; we were reared in castles, and are the children of yonder lords; tell us how the spell that is upon them may be broken!' And immediately the hunter turned from them with an angry look, poured out the milk upon the ground and went away with his empty goblet.

Loveleaves and Woodwender were sorry to see the rich cream spilled, but they remembered Lady Greensleeves's warning, and seeing they could do no better, each got a withered branch and began to help the lords, scratching up the ground with the sharp end, and planting acorns; but their fathers took no notice of them, nor all that they could say; and when the sun grew warm at noon they went again to drink at the running stream. Then there came through the oaks another hunter, older than the first, and clothed in yellow. About his neck there hung a silver bugle, and in his hand he carried an oaken goblet, carved with leaves and fruit, rimmed with silver and filled with mead to the brim. This hunter also asked them to drink, told them the stream was full of frogs, and asked them if they were not a young prince and princess dwelling in the woods for their pleasure? But when Woodwender and Loveleaves answered as before: 'We have promised to drink only running water and are the children of yonder lords: tell us how the spell may be broken!' – he turned from them with an angry look, poured out the mead and went his way.

All that afternoon the children worked beside their fathers, planting acorns with the withered branches; but the lords would mind neither them nor their words. And when the evening drew near they were very hungry, so the children divided their last cake, and when no persuasion would make the lords eat with them, they went to the banks of the stream, and began to eat and drink, though their hearts were heavy.

The sun was getting low, and the ravens were coming home to their nests in the high trees; but one, that seemed old and weary, alighted near them to drink at the stream. As they ate the raven lingered and picked up the small crumbs that fell.

'Brother,' said Loveleaves, 'this raven is surely hungry; let us give it a little bit, though it is our last cake.'

Woodwender agreed, and each gave a bit to the raven; but its great bill finished the morsels in a moment, and hopping nearer it looked them in the face by turns.

'The poor raven is still hungry,' said Woodwender, and he gave it another bit. When that was gobbled, it came to Loveleaves, who gave it a bit too, and so on till the raven had eaten the whole of their last cake.

'Well,' said Woodwender, 'at least we can have a drink.' But as they stooped to the water, there came through the oaks another hunter, older than the last and clothed in scarlet. About his neck there hung a golden bugle, and in his hand he carried a huge oaken goblet, carved with ears of corn and clusters of grapes, rimmed with gold and filled to the brim with wine. He also said:

'Leave this muddy water and drink with me. It is full of toads and not fit for such fair children. Surely you are from fairyland and were reared in its queen's palace!' But the children said:

'We will drink nothing but this water, and yonder lords are our fathers; tell us how the spell may be broken!' And the hunter turned from them with an angry look, poured out the wine on the grass and went his way.

When he was gone the old raven looked up into their faces and said:

'I have eaten your last cake, and I will tell you how the spell may be broken. Yonder is the sun, going down behind yon western trees. Before it sets, go to the lords, and tell them how their stewards used you, and made you herd hogs for Hardhold and Drypenny. When you see them listening, catch up their wooden spades, and keep them if you can till the sun goes down.'

Woodwender and Loveleaves thanked the raven, and where it flew they never stopped to see, but running to the lords began to tell as they were bidden. At first the lords would not listen, but as the children related how they had been made to sleep on straw, how they had been sent to herd

hogs in the wild pasture, and what trouble they had with the unruly swine, the acorn planting grew slower, and at last they dropped their spades. Then Woodwender, catching up his father's spade, ran to the stream and threw it in. Loveleaves did the same for the Lord of the White Castle. That moment the sun disappeared behind the western oaks, and the lords stood up, looking, like men just awakened, on the forest, on the sky, and on their children.

So this strange story has ended, for Woodwender and Loveleaves went home rejoicing with their fathers. Each lord returned to his castle, and all their tenants made merry. The fine toys and the silk clothes, the flower gardens and the best chambers, were taken from Hardhold and Drypenny, for the lords' children got them again; and the wicked stewards, with their cross boy and girl, were sent to herd swine and live in huts in the wild pasture, which everybody said became them better. The Lord of the White Castle never again wished to see the old woman that wove her own hair, and the Lord of the Grey Castle continued to be his friend. As for Woodwender and Loveleaves, they met with no more misfortunes, but grew up and were married and inherited the two castles and the broad lands of their fathers. Nor did they forget the lonely Lady Greensleeves, for it was known in the east country that she and her dwarf, Corner, always came to feast with them in the Christmas time, and at midsummer they always went to live with her in the great oak in the forest.

'Oh, mamma, if we had that oak!' said the Princess Greedalind.

'Where does it grow?' said Queen Wantall; but the chair was silent, and a noble lord and lady, clad in green velvet, flowered with gold, rose up and said:

'That's our story.'

'Excepting the tale of yesterday,' said King Winwealth, 'I have not heard such a story since my brother Wisewit went from me, and was lost in the forest. Gaygarters, the sixth of my pages, go and bring this maiden a pair of white silk hose with golden clocks on them.'

Queen Wantall and Princess Greedalind at this looked crosser than ever; but Gaygarters brought the white silk hose, and Snowflower, having dropped her curtsy and taken her seat, was carried once more to the kitchen, where they gave her a mattress that night, and next day she got the ends of choice dishes.

The feast, the music, and the dancing went on, so did the envies within and the clamours without the palace. In the evening King Winwealth fell again into low spirits after supper, and a message coming down from the banquet hall, the kitchen-maid told Snowflower to prepare herself and go up with her grandmother's chair, for his majesty wished to hear another story. Having washed her face and combed her

hair, put on her scarlet shoes and her gold-clocked hose, Snowflower went up as before, seated in her grandmother's chair, and after curtsying as usual to the king, the queen, the princess and the noble company, the little girl laid down her head, saying, 'Chair of my grandmother, tell me a story;' and a clear voice from under the cushion said:

'Listen to the story of the Greedy Shepherd.'

Chapter 4

THE GREEDY SHEPHERD

Once upon a time there lived in the south country two brothers, whose business it was to keep sheep on a great grassy plain, which was bounded on the one side by a forest and on the other by a chain of high hills. No one lived on that plain but shepherds, who dwelt in low cottages thatched with heath, and watched their sheep so carefully that no lamb was ever lost, nor had one of the shepherds ever travelled beyond the foot of the hills and the skirts of the forest.

There were none among them more careful than these two brothers, one of whom was called Clutch and the other Kind. Though brothers born, two men of countries far apart could not be more unlike in disposition. Clutch thought of nothing in this world but how to catch and keep some profit for himself, while Kind would have shared his last morsel with a hungry dog. This covetous mind made Clutch keep all his father's sheep when the old man was dead and gone, because he was the eldest brother, allowing Kind nothing but the place of a servant to help him in looking after them. Kind wouldn't quarrel with his brother for the sake of the sheep, so he helped him to keep them, and Clutch had all his own way. This made him agreeable. For some time the brothers lived peaceably in their father's cottage, which stood low and lonely under the shadow of a great sycamore tree, and kept their flock with pipe and crook on the grassy plain, till new troubles arose through Clutch's covetousness.

On that plain there was neither town nor city nor marketplace, where people might sell or buy; but the shepherds cared little for trade. The wool of their flocks made them clothes; their milk gave them butter and cheese. At feast times every family killed a lamb or so; their fields yielded them wheat for bread. The forest supplied them with firewood for winter; and every midsummer, which is the sheep-shearing time, traders from a certain far-off city came through it by an ancient way to purchase all the wool the shepherds could spare, and gave them in exchange either goods or money.

One midsummer it so happened that these traders praised the wool of Clutch's flock above all they found on the plain, and gave him the highest price for it. That was an unlucky happening for the sheep; from thenceforth Clutch thought he could never get enough wool off them. At the shearing time nobody clipped so close, and in spite of all Kind could do or say he left the poor sheep as bare as if they had been shaven; and as soon as the wool grew long enough to keep them warm, he was ready with the shears again – no matter how chilly might be the days, or how near the winter. Kind didn't like these doings, and many a debate they caused between him and his brother. Clutch always tried to persuade him that close clipping was good for the sheep, and Kind always strove to make him think he had got all the wool – so they were never done with disputes. Still Clutch sold the wool and stored up his profits, and one midsummer after another passed. The shepherds began to think him a rich man, and close clipping might have become the fashion, but for a strange thing which happened to his flock.

The wool had grown well that summer. He had taken two crops off them, and was thinking of a third – though the misty mornings of autumn were come, and the cold evenings made the shepherds put on their winter cloaks – when first the lambs, and then the ewes, began to stray away; and search as the brothers would, none of them was ever found again. Clutch blamed Kind with being careless, and watched with all his might. Kind knew it was not his fault, but he looked sharper than ever. Still the straying went on. The flocks grew smaller every day, and all the brothers could find out was, that the closest clipped were the first to go; and count the flock when they might, some were sure to be missed at the folding.

Kind grew tired of watching, and Clutch lost his sleep with vexation. The other shepherds, over whom he had boasted of his wool and his profits, were not sorry to see pride having a fall. Most of them pitied Kind, but all of them agreed that they had marvellous ill luck, and kept as far from them as they could for fear of sharing it. Still the flock melted away as the months wore on. Storms and cold weather never stopped them from straying, and when the spring came back nothing remained with Clutch and Kind but three old ewes, the quietest and lamest of their whole flock. They were watching these ewes one evening in the primrose time, when Clutch, who had never kept his eyes off them that day, said:

'Brother, there is wool to be had on their backs.'

'It is too little to keep them warm,' said Kind. 'The east wind still blows sometimes,' but Clutch was off to the cottage for the bag and shears.

Kind was grieved to see his brother so covetous, and to divert his mind he looked up at the great hills – it was a sort of comfort to him, ever since their losses began, to look at them evening and morning. Now their far-off heights were growing crimson with the setting sun, but as he looked three creatures like sheep scoured up a cleft in one of them as fleet as any deer; and when Kind turned he saw his brother coming with the bag and shears, but not a single ewe was to be seen. Clutch's first question was, what had become of them; and when Kind told him what he saw, the eldest brother scolded him with might and main for ever lifting his eyes off them.

'Much good the hills and the sunset do us,' said he, 'now that we have not a single sheep. The other shepherds will hardly give us room among them at shearing time or harvest; but for my part, I'll not stay on this plain to be despised for poverty. If you like to come with me, and be guided by my advice, we shall get service somewhere. I have heard my father say that there were great shepherds living in old times beyond the hills; let us go and see if they will take us for sheep boys.'

Kind would rather have stayed and tilled his father's wheat-field, hard by the cottage; but since his elder brother would go, he resolved to bear him company. Accordingly next morning Clutch took his bag and shears, Kind took his crook and pipe, and away they went over the plain and up the hills. All who saw them thought that they had lost their senses, for no shepherd had gone there for a hundred years, and nothing was to be seen but wide moorlands full of rugged rocks, and sloping up, it seemed, to the very sky. Kind persuaded his brother to take the direction the sheep had taken, but the ground was so rough and steep that after two hours' climbing they would gladly have turned back, if it had not been that their sheep were gone, and the shepherds would laugh at them.

By noon they came to the stony cleft, up which the three old ewes had scoured like deer; but both were tired and sat down to rest. Their feet were sore and their hearts were heavy; but as they sat there, there came a sound of music down the hills, as if a thousand shepherds had been playing on their tops. Clutch and Kind had never heard such music before. As they listened the soreness passed from their feet, and the heaviness from their hearts; and getting up they followed the sound up the cleft, and over a wide heath, covered with purple bloom, till at sunset they came to the hill top, and saw a broad pasture, where violets grew thick among the grass and thousands of snow-white sheep were feeding, while an old man sat in the midst of them, playing on his pipe. He wore a long coat, the colour of the holly leaves; his hair hung to his waist, and his beard to his knees; but both were as white as snow, and he had the countenance of one who had led a quiet life and known no cares nor losses.

'Good father,' said Kind, for his eldest brother hung back and was afraid, 'tell us what land is this, and where we can find service; for my brother and I are shepherds and can well keep flocks from straying, though we have lost our own.'

'These are the hill pastures,' said the old man, 'and I am the ancient shepherd. My flocks never stray, but I have employment for you. Which of you can shear best?'

'Good father,' said Clutch, taking courage, 'I am the closest shearer in all the plain country: you would not find as much wool as would make a thread on a sheep when I have done with it.'

'You are the man for my business,' replied the old shepherd. 'When the moon rises I will call the flock you have to shear. Till then sit down and rest, and take your supper out of my wallet.'

Clutch and Kind gladly sat down by him among the violets and, opening a leathern bag which hung by his side, the old man gave them cakes and cheese, and a horn cup to drink from a stream hard by. The brothers felt fit for any work after that meal, and Clutch rejoiced in his own mind at the chance he had got for showing his skill with the shears. 'Kind will see how useful it is to cut close,' he thought to himself; but they sat with the old man, telling him the news of the plain, till the sun went down and the moon rose, and all the snow-white sheep gathered and laid themselves down behind him. Then he took his pipe and played a merry tune, when immediately there was heard a great howling, and up the hills came a troop of shaggy wolves, with hair so long that their eyes could scarcely be seen. Clutch would

have fled for fear, but the wolves stopped, and the old man said to him:

'Rise, and shear – this flock of mine have too much wool on them.'

Clutch had never shorn wolves before, yet he couldn't think of losing the good service, and went forwards with a stout heart; but the first of the wolves showed its teeth, and all the rest raised such a howl the moment he came near them, that Clutch was glad to throw down his shears and run behind the old man for safety.

'Good father,' cried he, 'I will shear sheep, but not wolves.'

'They must be shorn,' said the old man, 'or you go back to the plains, and them after you; but whichever of you can shear them will get the whole flock.'

On hearing this Clutch began to exclaim on his hard fortune, and his brother who had brought him there to be hunted and devoured by wolves; but Kind, thinking that things could be no worse, caught up the shears he had thrown away in his fright, and went boldly up to the nearest wolf. To his great surprise the wild creature seemed to know him and stood quietly to be shorn, while the rest of the flock gathered round as if waiting their turn. Kind clipped neatly, but not too close, as he had wished his brother to do with the sheep, and heaped up the hair on one side. When he had done with one, another came forward, and Kind went on shearing by the bright moonlight till the whole flock was shorn. Then the old man said:

'You have done well; take the wool and the flock for your wages, return with them to the plain and if you please, take this little-worth brother of yours for a boy to keep them.'

Kind did not much like keeping wolves, but before he could make answer, they had all changed into the very sheep which had strayed away so strangely. All of them had grown fatter and thicker of fleece, and the hair he had cut off lay by his side, a heap of wool so fine and soft that its like had never been seen on the plain.

Clutch gathered it up in his empty bag, and glad was he to go back to the plain with his brother; for the old man sent them away with their flock, saying no man must see the dawn of day on that pasture but himself, for it was the ground of the fairies. So Clutch and Kind went home with great gladness. All the shepherds came to hear their wonderful story, and ever after liked to keep near them because they had such good luck. They keep sheep together till this day, but Clutch has grown less greedy, and Kind alone uses the shears.

With these words the voice ceased, and two shepherds, clad in grass-green and crowned with garlands, rose up and said:

'That's our story.'

'Mamma,' said Princess Greedalind, 'what a lovely playground that violet pasture would make for me!'

'What wool could be had off all those snow-white sheep!' said Queen Wantall. But King Winwealth said:

'Excepting yesterday's tale, and the one that went before it, I have not heard such a story as that since my brother Wisewit went from me and was lost in the forest. Spangledhose, the fifth of my pages, rise and bring this maiden a white satin gown.'

Snowflower took the white satin gown, thanked the king, curtseyed to the good company, and went down on her chair to the best kitchen. That night they gave her a new blanket, and next day she had a cold pie for dinner. The music, the feast, and the spite continued within the palace; so did the clamours without; and his majesty, falling into low spirits as usual after supper, one of the under-cooks told Snowflower that a message had come down from the highest banquet hall for her to go up with her grandmother's chair and tell another story. Snowflower accordingly dressed herself in the red shoes, the gold-clocked hose and the white satin gown. All the company were glad to see her and her chair coming, except the queen and the Princess Greedalind; and when the little girl had made her curtsy and laid down her head, saying, 'Chair of my grandmother, tell me a story,' the same clear voice said:

'Listen to the story of Fairyfoot.'

Chapter 5
The Story of Fairyfoot

Once upon a time there stood far away in the west country a town called Stumpinghame. It contained seven windmills, a royal palace, a market-place, and a prison, with every other convenience befitting the capital of a kingdom. A capital city was Stumpinghame, and its inhabitants thought it the only one in the world. It stood in the midst of a great plain, which for three leagues round its walls was covered with corn, flax and orchards. Beyond that lay a great circle of pasture land, seven leagues in breadth, and it was bounded on all sides by a forest so thick and old that no man in Stumpinghame knew its extent; and the opinion of the learned was that it reached to the end of the world.

There were strong reasons for this opinion. First, that forest was known to be inhabited time out of mind by the fairies, and no hunter cared to go beyond its borders – so all the west country believed it to be solidly full of old trees to the heart. Secondly, the people of Stumpinghame were no travellers – man, woman and child had feet so large and heavy that it was by no means convenient to carry them far. Whether it was the nature of the place or the people I cannot tell, but great feet had been the fashion there from time immemorial, and the higher the family the larger they were. It was therefore the aim of everybody above the degree of shepherds, and such-like rustics, to swell out and enlarge their feet by way of gentility; and so successful were they in these undertakings that, at a pinch, respectable people's slippers would have served for panniers.

Stumpinghame had a king of its own and his name was Stiffstep; his family was very ancient and large-footed. His subjects called him Lord of the World, and he made a speech to them every year concerning the grandeur of his mighty empire. His queen, Hammerheel, was the greatest beauty in Stumpinghame. Her majesty's shoe was not much less than a fishing-boat; their six children promised to be quite as handsome, and all went well with them till the birth of their seventh son.

For a long time nobody about the palace could understand what was the matter – the ladies-in-waiting looked so astonished, and the king so vexed; but at last it was whispered through the city that the queen's seventh child had been born with such miserably small feet that they resembled nothing ever heard of in Stumpinghame except the feet of the fairies.

The chronicles furnished no example of such an affliction ever before happening in the royal family. The common people thought it portended some great calamity to the city; the learned men began to write books about it, and all the relations of the king and queen assembled at the palace to mourn with them over their singular misfortune. The whole court and most of the citizens helped in this mourning, but when it had lasted seven days they all found out it was of no use. So the relations went to their homes, and the people took to their work. If the learned men's books were written, nobody ever read them; and to cheer up the queen's spirits, the young prince was sent privately out to the pasture lands, to be nursed among the shepherds.

The chief man there was called Fleecefold, and his wife's name was Rough Ruddy. They lived in a snug cottage with their son Blackthorn and their daughter Brownberry, and were thought great people because they kept the king's sheep. Moreover Fleecefold's family were known to be ancient, and Rough Ruddy boasted that she had the largest feet in all the pastures. The shepherds held them in high respect, and it grew still higher when the news spread that the king's seventh son had been sent to their cottage. People came from all quarters to see the young prince, and great were the lamentations over his misfortune in having such small feet.

The king and queen had given him fourteen names, beginning with Augustus – such being the fashion in that royal family; but the honest country people could not remember so many; besides, his feet were the most remarkable thing about the child, so with one accord they called him Fairyfoot. At first it was feared this might be high treason, but when no notice was taken by the king or his ministers, the shepherds concluded it was no harm, and the boy never had another name throughout the pastures. At court it was not thought polite to speak of him at all. They did not keep his birthday, and he was never sent for at Christmas because the queen and her ladies could not bear the sight. Once a year the under-most scullion was sent to see how he did, with a bundle of his next brother's cast-off clothes; and as the king grew old and cross it was said he had thoughts of disowning him.

So Fairyfoot grew in Fleecefold's cottage. Perhaps the country air made him fair and rosy – for all agreed that he would have been a handsome boy but for his small feet, with which nevertheless he learned to walk, and in time to run and to jump, thereby amazing everybody, for such doings were not known among the children of Stumpinghame. The news of court, however, travelled to the shepherds, and Fairyfoot was despised among them. The old people thought him unlucky; the children refused to play with him. Fleecefold was ashamed to have him in his cottage, but he durst not disobey the king's orders. Moreover Blackthorn wore most of the clothes brought by the scullion. At last Rough Ruddy found out that the sight of such horrid jumping would make her children vulgar; and, as soon as he was old enough, she sent Fairyfoot every day to watch some sickly sheep that grazed on a wild, weedy pasture, hard by the forest.

Poor Fairyfoot was often lonely and sorrowful; many a time he wished his feet would grow larger, or that people wouldn't notice them so much; and all the comfort he had was running and jumping by himself in the wild pasture, and thinking that none of the shepherds' children could do the like, for all their pride of their great feet.

Tired of this sport, he was lying in the shadow of a mossy rock one warm summer's noon, with the sheep feeding around, when a robin, pursued by a great hawk, flew into the old velvet cap which lay on the ground beside him. Fairyfoot covered it up, and the hawk, frightened by his shout, flew away.

'Now you may go, poor robin!' he said, opening the cap; but instead of the bird, out sprang a little man dressed in russet brown, and looking as if he were a hundred years old. Fairyfoot could not speak for astonishment, but the little man said:

'Thank you for your shelter, and be sure I will do as much for you. Call on me if you are ever in trouble; my name is Robin Goodfellow;' and darting off, he was out of sight in an instant. For days the boy wondered who that little man could be, but he told nobody, for the little man's feet were as small as his own, and it was clear he would be no favourite in Stumpinghame. Fairyfoot kept the story to himself, and at last midsummer came. That evening was a feast among the shepherds. There were bonfires on the hills, and fun in the villages. But Fairyfoot sat alone beside his sheepfold, for the children of his village had refused to let him dance with them about the bonfire, and he had gone there to bewail the size of his feet which came between him and so many good things. Fairyfoot had never felt so lonely in all his life, and remembering the little man, he plucked up spirit, and cried:

'Ho, Robin Goodfellow!'

'Here I am!' said a shrill voice at his elbow; and there stood the little man himself.

'I am very lonely, and no one will play with me, because my feet are not large enough,' said Fairyfoot.

'Come then and play with us,' said the little man. 'We lead the merriest lives in the world, and care for nobody's feet; but all companies have their own manners, and there are two things you must mind among us: first, do as you see the rest doing; and secondly, never speak of anything you may hear or see, for we and the people of this country have had no friendship ever since large feet came in fashion.'

'I will do that, and anything more you like,' said Fairyfoot; and the little man, taking his hand, led him over the pasture into the forest, and along a mossy path among old trees wreathed with ivy (he never knew how far), till they heard the sound of music and came upon a meadow where the moon shone as bright as day, and the flowers of the year – snowdrops, violets, primroses and cowslips – bloomed together in the thick grass. There were a crowd of little men and women, some clad in russet colour, but far more in green, dancing round a little well as clear as crystal. And under great rose trees which grew here and there in the meadow, companies were sitting round low tables covered with cups of milk, dishes of honey and carved

wooden flagons filled with clear red wine. The little man led Fairyfoot up to the nearest table, handed him one of the flagons and said:

'Drink to the good company!'

Wine was not very common among the shepherds of Stumpinghame, and the boy had never tasted such drink as that before; for scarcely had it gone down, when he forgot all his troubles – how Blackthorn and Brownberry wore his clothes, how Rough Ruddy sent him to keep the sickly sheep, and the children would not dance with him: in short, he forgot the whole misfortune of his feet, and it seemed to his mind that he was a king's son, and all was well with him. All the little people about the well cried, 'Welcome! welcome!' and everyone said: 'Come and dance with me!' So Fairyfoot was as happy as a prince, and drank milk and ate honey till the moon was low in the sky, and then the little man took him by the hand, and never stopped nor stayed till he was at his own bed of straw in the cottage corner.

Next morning Fairyfoot was not tired for all his dancing. Nobody in the cottage had missed him, and he went out with the sheep as usual; but every night all that summer, when the shepherds were safe in bed, the little man came and took him away to dance in the forest. Now he did not care to play with the shepherds' children, nor grieve that his father and mother had forgotten him, but watched the sheep all day, singing to himself or plaiting rushes; and when the sun went down, Fairyfoot's heart rejoiced at the thought of meeting that merry company.

The wonder was that he was never tired nor sleepy, as people are apt to be

who dance all night; but before the summer was ended Fairyfoot found out the reason. One night, when the moon was full and the last of the ripe corn rustling in the fields, Robin Goodfellow came for him as usual, and away they went to the flowery green. The fun there was high, and Robin was in haste. So he only pointed to the carved cup from which Fairyfoot every night drank the clear red wine.

'I am not thirsty, and there is no use losing time,' thought the boy to himself, and he joined the dance; but never in all his life did Fairyfoot find such hard work as to keep pace with the company. Their feet seemed to move like lightning; the swallows did not fly so fast or turn so quickly. Fairyfoot did his best, for he never gave in easily, but at length, his breath and strength being spent, the boy was glad to steal away and sit down behind a mossy oak, where his eyes closed for very weariness. When he awoke the dance was nearly over, but two little ladies clad in green talked beside him.

'What a beautiful boy!' said one of them. 'He is worthy to be a king's son. Only see what handsome feet he has!'

'Yes,' said the other, with a laugh that sounded spiteful; 'they are just like the feet Princess Maybloom had before she washed them in the Growing Well. Her father has sent far and wide throughout the whole country searching for a doctor to make them small again, but nothing in this world can do it except the water of the Fair Fountain, and none but I and the nightingales know where it is.'

'One would not care to let the like be known,' said the first little lady; 'there would come such crowds of these great coarse creatures of mankind, nobody would have peace for leagues round. But you will surely send word to the sweet princess! – she was so kind to our birds and butterflies, and danced so like one of ourselves!'

'Not I, indeed!' said the spiteful fairy. 'Her old skinflint of a father cut down the cedar which I loved best in the whole forest, and made a chest of it to hold his money in; besides, I never liked the princess – everybody praised her so. But come, we shall be too late for the last dance.'

When they were gone, Fairyfoot could sleep no more with astonishment. He did not wonder at the fairies admiring his feet, because their own were much the same; but it amazed him that Princess Maybloom's father should be troubled at hers growing large. Moreover he wished to see that same princess and her country, since there were really other places in the world than Stumpinghame.

When Robin Goodfellow came to take him home as usual he durst not let him know that he had overheard anything: but never was the boy so unwilling to get up as on that morning, and all day he was so weary that in the afternoon Fairyfoot fell asleep, with his head on a dump of rushes. It was seldom that anyone thought of looking after him and the sickly sheep; but it so happened that towards evening the old shepherd, Fleecefold, thought he would see how things went on in the pastures. The shepherd had a bad temper and a thick staff, and no sooner did he catch sight of Fairyfoot sleeping and his flock straying away, than shouting all the ill names he could remember, in a voice which woke up the boy, he ran after him as fast as his great feet would allow; while Fairyfoot, seeing no other shelter from his fury, fled into the forest, and never stopped nor stayed till he reached the banks of a little stream.

Thinking it might lead him to the fairies' dancing ground, he followed that stream for many an hour, but it wound away into the heart of the forest, flowing through dells, falling over mossy rocks and at last leading Fairyfoot, when he was tired and the night had fallen, to a grove of great rose trees, with the moon shining on it as bright as day, and thousands of nightingales singing in the branches. In the midst of that grove was a clear spring, bordered with banks of lilies, and Fairyfoot sat down by it to rest himself and listen. The singing was so sweet he could have listened for ever, but as he sat the nightingales left off their songs, and began to talk together in the silence of the night.

'What boy is that,' said one on a branch above him, 'who sits so lonely by the Fair Fountain? He cannot have come from Stumpinghame with such small and handsome feet.'

'No, I'll warrant you,' said another, 'he has come from the west country. How in the world did he find the way?'

'How simple you are!' said a third nightingale. 'What had he to do but follow the ground-ivy which grows over height and hollow, bank and bush, from the lowest gate of the king's kitchen garden to the root of this rose tree? He looks a wise boy, and I hope he will keep the secret, or we shall have all the west country here, dabbling in our fountain, and leaving us no rest to either talk or sing.'

Fairyfoot sat in great astonishment at this discourse, but by and by, when the talk ceased and the songs began, he thought it might be as well for him to follow the ground-ivy, and see the Princess Maybloom, not to speak of

getting rid of Rough Ruddy, the sickly sheep, and the crusty old shepherd. It was a long journey; but he went on, eating wild berries by day, sleeping in the hollows of old trees by night, and never losing sight of the ground-ivy, which led him over height and hollow, bank and bush, out of the forest and along a noble high road, with fields and villages on every side, to a great city, and a low old-fashioned gate of the king's kitchen garden, which was thought too mean for the scullions and had not been opened for seven years.

There was no use knocking – the gate was overgrown with tall weeds and moss; so, being an active boy, he climbed over, and walked through the garden, till a white fawn came frisking by, and he heard a soft voice saying sorrowfully:

'Come back, come back, my fawn! I cannot run and play with you now, my feet have grown so heavy;' and looking round he saw the loveliest princess in the world, dressed in snow white, and wearing a wreath of roses on her golden hair; but walking slowly, as the great people did in

Stumpinghame, for her feet were as large as the best of them.

After her came six young ladies, dressed in white and walking slowly, for they could not go before the princess; but Fairyfoot was amazed to see that their feet were as small as his own. At once he guessed that this must be the Princess Maybloom, and made her a humble bow, saying:

'Royal princess, I have heard of your trouble because your feet have grown large: in my country that's all the fashion. For seven years past I have been wondering what would make mine grow, to no purpose; but I know of a certain fountain that will make yours smaller and finer than ever they were, if the king, your father, gives you leave to come with me, accompanied by two of your maids that are the least given to talking, and the most prudent officer in all his household; for it would grievously offend the fairies and the nightingales to make that fountain known.'

When the princess heard that, she danced for joy in spite of her large feet, and she and her six maids brought Fairyfoot before the king and queen, where they sat in their palace hall, with all the courtiers paying their morning compliments. The lords were very much astonished to see a ragged, barefooted boy brought in

among them, and the ladies thought Princess Maybloom must have gone mad; but Fairyfoot, making a humble reverence, told his message to the king and queen, and offered to set out with the princess that very day. At first the king would not believe that there could be any use in his offer, because so many great physicians had failed to give any relief. The courtiers laughed Fairyfoot to scorn, the pages wanted to turn him out for an impudent impostor, and the prime minister said he ought to be put to death for high treason.

Fairyfoot wished himself safe in the forest again, or even keeping the sickly sheep; but the queen, being a prudent woman, said:

'I pray your majesty to notice what fine feet this boy has. There may be some truth in his story. For the sake of our only daughter, I will choose two maids who talk the least of all our train, and my chamberlain, who is the most discreet officer in our household. Let them go with the princess: who knows but our sorrow may be lessened?'

After some persuasion the king consented, though all his councillors advised the contrary. So the two silent maids, the discreet chamberlain and her fawn, which would not stay behind, were sent with Princess Maybloom, and they all set out after dinner. Fairyfoot had hard work guiding them along the track of the ground-ivy. The maids and the chamberlain did not like the brambles and rough roots of the forest – they thought it hard to eat berries and sleep in hollow trees; but the princess went on with good courage, and at last they reached the grove of rose trees, and the spring bordered with lilies.

The chamberlain washed – and though his hair had been grey and his face wrinkled, the young courtiers envied his beauty for years after. The maids washed – and from that day they were esteemed the fairest in all the palace. Lastly, the princess washed also – it could make her no fairer, but the moment her feet touched the water they grew less, and when she had washed and dried them three times, they were as small and finely shaped as Fairyfoot's own. There was great joy among them, but the boy said sorrowfully:

'Oh, if there had been a well in the world to make my feet large, my father and mother would not have cast me off, nor sent me to live among the shepherds.'

'Cheer up your heart,' said the Princess Maybloom; 'if you want large feet there is a well in this forest that will do it. Last summer time I came with my father and his foresters to see a great cedar cut down, of which he meant to make a money chest. While they were busy with the cedar, I saw a bramble branch covered with berries. Some were ripe and some were green, but it was the longest bramble that ever grew; for the sake of the berries I went on and on to its root, which grew hard by a muddy looking well with banks of dark green moss, in the deepest part of the forest. The day was warm and dry, and my feet were sore with the rough ground, so I took off my scarlet shoes, and washed my feet in the well; but as I washed they grew larger every minute, and nothing could ever make them less again. I have seen the bramble this day; it is not far off, and as you have shown me the Fair Fountain, I will show you the Growing Well.'

Up rose Fairyfoot and Princess Maybloom, and went together till they found the bramble, and came to where its root grew, hard by the muddy-looking well with banks of dark green moss in the deepest dell of the forest. Fairyfoot sat down to wash, but at that minute he heard a sound of music, and knew it was the fairies going to their dancing ground.

'If my feet grow large,' said the boy to himself, 'how shall I dance with them?' So, rising quickly, he took the Princess Maybloom by the hand. The fawn followed them; the maids and the chamberlain followed it, and all followed the music through the forest. At last they came to the flowery green. Robin Goodfellow welcomed the company for Fairyfoot's sake, and gave everyone a drink of the fairies' wine. So they danced there from sunset till the grey morning, and nobody was tired; but before the lark sang Robin Goodfellow took them all safe home, as he used to take Fairyfoot.

There was great joy that day in the palace because Princess Maybloom's feet were made small again. The king gave Fairyfoot all manner of fine clothes and rich jewels; and when they heard his wonderful story, he and the queen asked him to live with them and be their son. In process of time Fairyfoot and Princess Maybloom were married, and still live happily. When they go to visit at Stumpinghame, they always wash their feet in the Growing Well, lest the royal family might think them a disgrace, but when they come back, they make haste to the Fair Fountain; and the fairies and the nightingales are great friends to them, as well as the maids and the chamberlain, because they have told nobody about it, and there is peace and quiet yet in the grove of rose trees.

Here the voice out of the cushion ceased, and two that wore crowns of gold, and were clothed in cloth of silver, rose up and said:

'That's our story.'

'Mamma,' said Princess Greedalind, 'if we could find out that Fair Fountain and keep it all to ourselves!'

'Yes, my daughter, and the Growing Well to wash our money in,' replied Queen Wantall. But King Winwealth said:

'Excepting yesterday's tale, and the two that went before it, I have not heard such a story since my brother Wisewit went from me and was lost in the forest. Silverspurs, the fourth of my pages, go and bring this maiden a pearl necklace.'

Snowflower received the necklace accordingly, gave her thanks, made her curtsy and went down on her grandmother's chair to the servants' hall. That night they gave her a down pillow, and next day she dined on a roast chicken. The feasting within and the clamour without went on as the days before: King Winwealth fell into his accustomed low spirits after supper, and sent down a message for Snowflower, which was told her by the master cook. So the little girl went up in her grandmother's chair, with red shoes, the clocked hose, the white satin gown and the pearl necklace on. All the company welcomed her with joyful looks, and no sooner had she made her curtsy and laid down her head, saying, 'Chair of my grandmother, tell me a story,' than the clear voice from under the cushion said:

'Listen to the story of Childe Charity.'

70

Chapter 6

THE STORY OF
CHILDE CHARITY

Once upon a time there lived in the west country a little girl who had neither father nor mother; they both died when she was very young, and left their daughter to the care of her uncle, who was the richest farmer in all that country. He had houses and lands, flocks and herds, many servants to work about his house and fields, a wife who had brought him a great dowry, and two fair daughters. All their neighbours, being poor, looked up to the family – insomuch that they imagined themselves great people. The father and mother were as proud as peacocks; the daughters thought themselves the greatest beauties in the world, and not one of the family would speak civilly to anybody they thought low.

Now it happened that though she was their near relation, they had this opinion of the orphan girl, partly because she had no fortune, and partly because of her humble, kindly disposition. It was said that the more needy and despised any creature was, the more ready was she to befriend it: on which account the people of the west country called her Childe Charity, and if she had any other name, I never heard it. Childe Charity was thought very mean in that proud house. Her uncle would not own her for his niece; her cousins would not keep her company; and her aunt sent her to work in the dairy, and to sleep in the back garret, where they kept all sorts of lumber and dry herbs for the winter. All the servants learned the same tune, and Childe Charity had more work than rest among them. All the day she scoured pads, scrubbed dishes and washed crockery-ware; but every night she slept in the back garret as sound as a princess could in her palace chamber.

Her uncle's house was large and white, and stood among green meadows by a river's side. In front it had a porch covered with a vine; behind, it had a farmyard and high granaries. Within there were two parlours for the rich, and two kitchens for the poor, which the neighbours thought wonderfully grand; and one day in the harvest season, when this rich farmer's corn had been all cut down and housed, he condescended so far as to invite them to a harvest supper. The west country people came in their holiday clothes and best behaviour. Such heaps of cakes and cheese, such baskets of apples and barrels of ale, had never been at a feast before; and they were making merry in kitchen and parlour, when a poor old woman came to the back door, begging for broken victuals and a night's lodging. Her clothes were coarse and ragged; her hair was scanty and grey; her back was bent; her teeth were gone. She had a squinting eye, a clubbed foot, and crooked fingers. In short, she was the poorest and ugliest old woman that ever came begging. The first who saw her was the kitchen-maid, and she ordered her to be gone for an ugly witch. The next was the herd boy, and he threw her a bone over his shoulder; but Childe Charity, hearing the noise, came out from her seat at the foot of the lowest table, and asked the old woman to take her share of the supper and sleep that night in her bed in the back garret. The old woman sat down without a word of thanks. All the company laughed at Childe Charity for giving her bed and her supper to a beggar. Her proud cousins said it was just like her mean spirit, but Childe Charity did not mind them. She scraped the pots for her supper that night and slept on a sack among the lumber, while the old woman rested in her warm bed; and next morning, before the little girl awoke, she was up and gone, without so much as saying 'Thank you' or 'Good morning'.

That day all the servants were sick after the feast, and mostly cross too – so you may judge how civil they were; when, at supper time, who should come to the back door but the old woman, again asking for broken victuals and a night's lodging. No one would listen to her or give her a morsel, till Childe Charity rose from her seat at the foot of the lowest table and kindly asked her to take her supper and sleep in her bed in the back garret. Again the old woman sat down without a word. Childe Charity scraped the pots for her supper and slept on the sack. In the morning the old woman was gone; but for six nights after, as sure as the supper was spread, there was she at the back door, and the little girl regularly asked her in.

Childe Charity's aunt said she would let her get enough of beggars. Her cousins made continual game of what they called her genteel visitor. Sometimes the old woman said, 'Child, why don't you make this bed softer? And why are your blankets so thin?' But she never gave her a word of thanks nor a civil 'Good morning'. At last, on the ninth night from her first coming, when Childe Charity was getting used to scraping the pots and sleeping on the sack, the old woman's accustomed knock came on the door, and there she stood with an ugly ashy-coloured dog, so stupid-looking and clumsy that no herd boy would keep him.

'Good evening, my little girl,' she said when Childe Charity opened the door. 'I will not have your supper and bed tonight – I am going on a long journey to see a friend; but here is a dog of mine, whom nobody in all the west country will keep for me. He is a little cross and not very handsome; but I leave him to your care till the shortest day in all the year. Then you and I will count for his keeping.'

When the old woman had said the last word, she set off with such speed that Childe Charity lost sight of her in a minute. The ugly dog began to fawn upon her, but he snarled at everybody else. The servants said he was a disgrace to the house. The proud cousins wanted him drowned, and it was with great trouble that Childe Charity got leave to keep him in an old ruined cowhouse. Ugly and cross as the dog was, he fawned on her, and the old woman had left him to her care. So the little girl gave him part of all her meals, and when the hard frost came took him privately to her own back garret, because the cow-house was damp and cold in the long nights. The dog lay quietly on some straw in a corner. Childe Charity slept soundly, but every morning the servants would say to her:

'What great light and fine talking was that in your back garret?'

'There was no light but the moon shining in through the shutterless window, and no talk that I heard,' said Childe Charity, and she thought they must have been dreaming; but night after night, when any of them awoke in the dark and silent hour that comes before the morning, they saw a light brighter and clearer than the Christmas fire, and heard voices like those of lords and ladies in the back garret.

Partly from fear, and partly from laziness, none of the servants would rise to see what might be there; till at length, when the winter nights were at the longest, the little parlour-maid, who did least work and got most favour because she gathered news for her mistress, crept out of bed when all the rest were sleeping and set herself to watch at a crevice of the door. She saw the dog lying quietly in the corner, Childe Charity sleeping soundly in her bed, and the moon shining through the shutterless window. But an hour before daybreak there came a glare of lights, and a sound of far-off bugles. The window opened, and in marched a troop of little men clothed in crimson and gold and bearing every man a torch, till the room looked bright as day. They marched up with great reverence to the dog, where he lay on the straw, and the most richly clothed among them said:

'Royal prince, we have prepared the banquet hall. What will your highness please that we do next?'

'You have done well,' said the dog. 'Now prepare the feast and see that all things be in our first fashion: for the princess and I mean to bring a stranger who never feasted in our halls before.'

'Your highness's commands shall be obeyed,' said the little man, making another reverence; and he and his company passed out of the window. By and by there was another glare of lights, and a sound like far-off flutes. The window opened, and there came in a company of little ladies clad in rose-coloured velvet and carrying each a crystal lamp. They also walked with great reverence up to the dog, and the gayest among them said:

'Royal prince, we have prepared the tapestry. What will your highness please that we do next?'

'You have done well,' said the dog. 'Now prepare the robes and let all things be in our first fashion: for the princess and I will bring with us a stranger who never feasted in our halls before.'

'Your highness's commands shall be obeyed,' said the little lady, making a low curtsy; and she and her company passed out through the window, which closed quietly behind them. The dog stretched himself out upon the straw, the little girl turned in her sleep, and the moon

shone in on the back garret. The parlour-maid was so much amazed, and so eager to tell this great story to her mistress, that she could not close her eyes that night, and was up before cock-crow; but when she told it, her mistress called her a silly wench to have such foolish dreams, and scolded her so that the parlour-maid durst not mention what she had seen to the servants. Nevertheless Childe Charity's aunt thought there might be something in it worth knowing; so next night, when all the house were asleep, she crept out of bed and set herself to watch at the back garret door. There she saw exactly what the maid told her – the little men with the torches, and the little ladies with the crystal lamps, come in making great reverence to the dog, and the same words pass, only he said to the one, 'Now prepare the presents,' and to the other, 'Prepare the jewels;' and when they were gone the dog stretched himself on the straw, Childe Charity turned in her sleep and the moon shone in on the back garret.

The mistress could not close her eyes any more than the maid from eagerness to tell the story. She woke up Childe Charity's rich uncle before cock-crow; but when he heard it, he laughed at her for a foolish woman and advised her not to repeat the like before the neighbours, lest they should think she had lost her senses. The mistress could say no more, and the day passed; but that night the master thought he would like to see what went on in the back garret: so when all the house were asleep he slipped out of bed and set himself to watch at the crevice in the door. The same thing happened again that the maid and the mistress saw: the little men in crimson with their torches, and the little ladies in rose-coloured velvet with their lamps, came in at the window and made a humble reverence to the ugly dog, the one saying, 'Royal prince, we have prepared the presents,' and the other, 'Royal prince, we have prepared the jewels;' and the dog said to them all: 'You have done well. Tomorrow come and meet me and the princess with horses and chariots, and let all things be in our first fashion: for we will bring a stranger from this house who has never travelled with us nor feasted in our halls before.'

The little men and the little ladies said: 'Your highness's commands shall be obeyed.' When they had gone out through the window the ugly dog stretched himself out on the straw, Childe Charity turned in her sleep and the moon shone in on the back garret.

The master could not close his eyes any more than the maid or the mistress for thinking of this strange sight. He remembered to have heard his grandfather say that somewhere near his meadows there lay a path leading to the fairies' country, and the haymakers used to see it shining through the grey summer morning as the fairy bands went home. Nobody had heard or seen the like for many years; but the master concluded that the doings in his back garret must be a fairy business and the ugly dog a person of great account. His chief wonder was, however, what visitor the fairies intended to take from his house; and after thinking the matter over he was sure it must be one of his daughters – they were so handsome and had such fine clothes.

Accordingly, Childe Charity's rich uncle made it his first business that morning to get ready a breakfast of roast mutton for the ugly dog, and carry it to him in the old cow-house; but not a morsel would the dog taste. On the contrary, he snarled at the master, and would have bitten him if he had not run away with his mutton.

'The fairies have strange ways,' said the master to himself; but he called his daughters privately, bidding them dress themselves in their best, for he could not say which of them might be called into great company before nightfall. Childe Charity's proud cousins, hearing this, put on the richest of their silks and laces and strutted like peacocks from kitchen to parlour all day, waiting for the call their father spoke of, while the little girl scoured and scrubbed in the dairy. They were in very bad humour when night fell and nobody had come; but just as the family were sitting down to supper the ugly dog began to bark, and the old woman's knock was heard at the back door. Childe Charity opened it, and was going to offer her bed and supper as usual, when the old woman said:

'This is the shortest day in all the year, and I am going home to hold a feast after my travels. I see you have taken good care of my dog, and now if you will come with me to my house, he and I will do our best to entertain you. Here is our company.'

As the old woman spoke there was a sound of far-off flutes and bugles, then a glare of lights; and a great company, clad so grandly that they shone with gold and jewels, came in open chariots, covered with gilding and drawn by snow-white horses. The first and finest of the chariots was empty. The old woman led Childe Charity to it by the hand, and the ugly dog jumped in before her. The proud cousins in all their finery had by this time come to the door, but nobody wanted them; and no sooner were the old woman and her dog within the chariot than a marvellous change passed over them, for the ugly old woman turned at once to a beautiful young princess with long, yellow curls and a robe of green and gold, while the ugly dog at her side started up a fair young prince, with nut-brown hair and a robe of purple and silver.

'We are,' said they, as the chariots drove on, and the little girl sat astonished, 'a prince and princess of Fairyland, and there was a wager between us whether or not there were good people still to be found in these false and greedy times. One said "Yes", and the other said "No"; and I have lost,' said the prince, 'and must pay the feast and presents.'

Childe Charity never heard any more of that story. Some of the farmer's household who were looking after them through the moonlight night said the chariots had gone one way across the meadows, some said they had gone another, and till this day they cannot agree upon the direction. But Childe Charity went with that noble company into a country such as she had never seen – for primroses covered all the ground and the light was always like that of a summer evening. They took her to a royal palace, where there was nothing but feasting and dancing for seven days. She had robes of pale green velvet to wear and slept in a chamber inlaid with ivory. When the feast was done the prince and princess gave her such heaps of gold and jewels that she could not carry them, but they gave her a chariot to go home in, drawn by six white horses; and on the seventh night, which happened to be Christmas time, when the farmer's family had settled in their own minds that she would never come back and were sitting down to supper, they heard the sound of her coachman's bugle, and saw her alight with all the jewels and gold at the very back door where she had brought in the ugly old woman. The fairy chariot drove away, and never came back to the farmhouse after. But Childe Charity scrubbed and scoured no more, for she grew to be a great lady, even in the eyes of her proud cousins.

Here the voice out of the cushion ceased, and one, with a fair face and a robe of pale green velvet, rose from among the company, and said:

'That's my story.'

'Mamma,' said Princess Greedalind, 'if we had some of those fine chariots!'

'Yes, my daughter,' answered Queen Wantall, 'and the gold and jewels too!' But King Winwealth said:

'Excepting yesterday's story, and the three that went before it, I have not heard such a tale since my brother Wisewit went from me, and was lost in the forest. Highjinks, the third of my pages, go and bring this maiden a crimson velvet hat.'

Snowflower took the hat and thanked the king, made her curtsy, and went down on her grandmother's chair to the housekeeper's parlour. Her blanket was covered with a patchwork quilt that night; next day she had roast turkey and meat for dinner. But the feast went on in the palace hall with the usual spites and envies; the clamour and complaints at the gate were still heard above all the music; and King Winwealth fell into his wonted low spirits as soon as the supper was over. As usual, a message came down from the banquet hall, and the chief butler told Snowflower that she and her chair were wanted to tell King Winwealth a story. So she went up with all the presents on, even to the crimson hat, made her curtsy to the good company, and had scarcely said, 'Chair of my grandmother, tell me a story,' when the voice from under the cushion said:

'Listen to the story of Sour and Civil.'

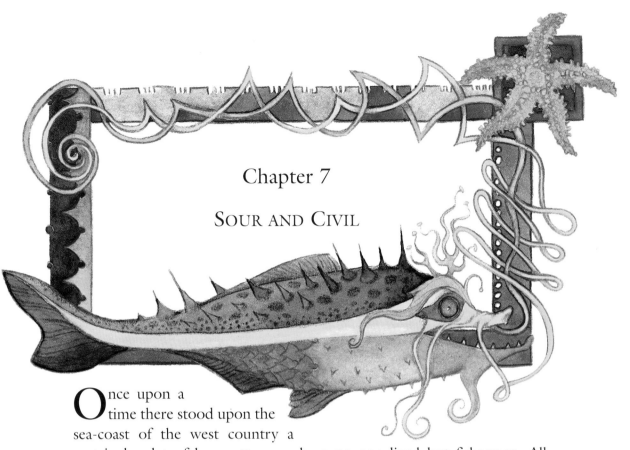

Chapter 7

SOUR AND CIVIL

Once upon a time there stood upon the sea-coast of the west country a certain hamlet of low cottages, where no one lived but fishermen. All round it was a broad beach of snow-white sand, where nothing was to be seen but gulls and cormorants, and long tangled seaweeds cast up by the tide that came and went night and day, summer and winter. There was no harbour nor port on all that shore. Ships passed by at a distance, with their white sails set, and on the land side there lay wide grassy downs, where peasants lived and shepherds fed their flocks. The fishermen thought themselves as well off as any people in that country. Their families never wanted for plenty of herrings and mackerel; and what they had to spare the landsmen bought from them at certain village markets on the downs, giving them in exchange butter, cheese and corn.

The two best fishermen in that village were the sons of two old widows who had no other children, and happened to be near neighbours. Their family names were short, for they called the one Sour and the other Civil. There was no relationship between them that ever I heard of; but they had only one boat and always fished together, though their names expressed the difference of their humours – for Civil never used a hard word where a soft one would do, and when Sour was not snarling at somebody, he was sure to be grumbling at everything.

Nevertheless they agreed wonderfully, and were lucky fishers. Both were strong, active, and of good courage. On winter's night or summer's morning they would steer out to sea far beyond the boats of their neighbours, and never came home without some fish to cook and some to spare. Their mothers were proud of them, each in her own fashion – for the saying held good, 'Like mother, like son.' Dame Civil thought the whole world didn't hold a better than her son; and her boy was the only creature at whom Dame Sour didn't scold and frown. The hamlet was divided in opinion concerning the young fishermen. Some thought Civil the best; some said, without Sour he would catch nothing. So things went on, till one day about the fall of winter, when mists were gathering darkly on sea and sky and the air was chill and frosty, all the boatmen of the hamlet went out to fish, and so did Sour and Civil.

That day they had not their usual luck. Cast their net where they would, not a single fish came in. Their neighbours caught boatfuls, and went home, Sour said, laughing at them. But when the sea was growing crimson with the sunset their nets were empty, and they were tired. Civil himself did not like to go home without fish – it would damage the high repute they had gained in the village. Besides, the sea was calm and the evening fair, and as a last attempt they steered still farther out, and Sour and Civil cast their nets beside a rock which rose rough and grey above the water, and was called the Merman's Seat – from an old report that the fishermen's fathers had seen the mermen, or sea people, sitting there on moonlight nights. Nobody believed that rumour now, but the villagers did not like to fish there. The water was said to be deep beyond measure, and sudden squalls were apt to trouble it; but Sour and Civil were right glad to see by the moving of their lines that there was something in their net, and gladder still when they found it so heavy that all their strength was required to draw it up. Scarcely had they landed it on the Merman's Seat, when their joy was changed to disappointment, for besides a few starved mackerel, the net contained nothing but a monstrous ugly fish as long as Civil (who was taller than Sour), with a huge snout, a long beard, and a skin covered with prickles.

'Such a horrid ugly creature!' said Sour, as they shook it out of the net on the rough rock and gathered up the mackerel. 'We needn't fish here any more. How they will mock us in the village for staying out so late, and bringing home so little!'

'Let us try again,' said Civil, as he set his creel of mackerel in the boat.

'Not another cast will I make tonight;' and what more Sour would have said, was cut short by the great fish, for, looking round at them, it spoke out:

'I suppose you don't think me worth taking home in your dirty boat; but I can tell you that if you were down in my country, neither of you would be thought fit to keep me company.'

Sour and Civil were terribly astonished to hear the fish speak. The first could not think of a cross word to say, but Civil made answer in his accustomed manner.

'Indeed, my lord, we beg your pardon, but our boat is too light to carry such a fish as you.'

'You do well to call me lord,' said the fish, 'for so I am, though it was hard to expect you could have known my quality in this dress. However, help me off the rock, for I must go home; and for your civility I will give you my daughter in marriage, if you will come and see me this day twelvemonth.'

Civil helped the great fish off the rock as respectfully as his fear would allow him. Sour was so terrified at the whole transaction that he said not a word till they got safe home; but from that day forward, when he wanted to put Civil down, it was his custom to tell him and his mother that he would get no wife but the ugly fish's daughter.

Old Dame Sour heard this story from her son, and told it over the whole village. Some people wondered, but the most part laughed at it as a good joke; and Civil and his mother were never known to be angry but on that occasion. Dame Civil advised her son never to fish with Sour again; and as the boat happened to be his, Civil got an old skiff which one of the fishermen was going to break up for firewood, and cobbled it up for himself.

In that skiff he went to sea alone all the winter, and all the summer; but though Civil was brave and skilful, he could catch little, because his boat was bad – and everybody but his mother began to think him of no value. Sour having the good boat got a new comrade, and had the praise of being the best fisherman.

Poor Civil's heart was getting low as the summer wore away. The fish had grown scarce on that coast, and the fishermen had to steer farther out to sea. One evening when he had toiled all day and caught nothing, Civil

thought he would go farther too, and try his fortune beside the Merman's rock. The sea was calm and the evening fair; Civil did not remember that it was the very day on which his troubles began by the great fish talking to him twelve months before. As he neared the rock the sun was setting, and much astonished was the fisherman to see upon it three fair ladies, with sea-green gowns and strings of great pearls wound round their long fair hair; two of them were waving their hands to him. They were the tallest and stateliest ladies he had ever seen; but Civil could perceive as he came nearer that there was no colour in their cheeks, that their hair had a strange bluish shade, like that of deep sea-water, and there was a fiery light in their eyes that frightened him. The third, who was less of stature, did not notice him at all, but kept her eyes fixed on the setting sun. Though her look was mournful, Civil could see that there was a faint rosy bloom on her cheek, that her hair was a golden yellow, and her eyes were mild and clear like those of his mother.

'Welcome, welcome, noble fisherman!' cried the two ladies. 'Our father has sent us for you to visit him.' And with one bound they leaped into his boat, bringing with them the smaller lady, who said:

'Oh, bright sun and brave sky that I see so seldom!' But Civil heard no more, for his boat went down miles deep in the sea, and he thought himself drowning; but one lady had caught him by the right arm, and the other by the left, and they pulled him into the mouth of a rocky cave, where there was no water. On they went, still down and down, as if on a

steep hillside. The cave was very long, but it grew wider
as they came to the bottom. Then Civil saw a faint light,
and walked out with his fair company into the country
of the sea people. In that land there grew neither grass
nor flowers, bushes nor trees, but the ground was
covered with bright-coloured shells and pebbles.
There were hills of marble, and rocks of spar; and
over all a cold blue sky with no sun, but a
light, clear and silvery as that of the harvest
moon. The fisherman could see no smoking
chimneys, but there were grottoes in the
sparry rocks and halls in the marble hills,
where lived the sea people – with whom, as
old stories say, fishermen and mariners used
to meet on lonely capes and headlands in
the simple times of the world.

Forth they came in all directions to see the
stranger. Mermen with long white beards,
and mermaids such as walk with the
fishermen, all clad in sea-green, and
decorated with strings of pearls; but
everyone with the same colourless face and
the same wild light in their eyes. The
mermaids led Civil up one of the marble hills
to a great cavern with halls and chambers like
a palace. Their floors were of alabaster, their
walls of porphyry, and their ceilings inlaid with
coral. Thousands of crystal lamps lit the palace.
There were seats and tables hewn out of shining
spar, and a great company sat feasting; but what
most amazed Civil was the quantity of cups, flagons
and goblets, made of gold and silver, of such
different shapes and patterns that they seemed
to have been gathered from all the
countries in the world. In the chief hall
there sat a merman on a stately chair,
with more jewels than all the rest about

him. Before him the mermaids brought Civil, saying:

'Father, here is our guest.'

'Welcome, noble fisherman!' cried the merman, in a voice which Civil remembered with terror, for it was that of the great ugly fish. 'Welcome to our halls! Sit down and feast with us, and then choose which of my daughters you will have for a bride.'

Civil had never felt himself so thoroughly frightened in all his life. How was he to get home to his mother? And what would the old dame think when the dark night came without bringing him home? There was no use in talking – Civil had wisdom enough to see that: he therefore tried to take things quietly; and, having thanked the merman for his invitation, took the seat assigned him on his right hand. Civil was hungry with the long day at sea, but there was no want of fare on that table: meats and wines, such as he had never tasted, were set before him in the richest of golden dishes: but hungry as he was, the fisherman perceived that everything there had the taste and smell of the sea.

If the fisherman had been the lord of lands and castles he would not have been treated with more respect. The two mermaids sat by him – one filled his plate, another filled his goblet; but the third only looked at him in a stealthy, warning way when nobody perceived her. Civil soon finished his share of the feast, and then the merman showed him all the splendours of his cavern. The halls were full of company, some feasting, some dancing, and some playing all manner of games, and in every hall was the same abundance of gold and silver vessels; but Civil was most astonished when the merman brought him to a marble chamber full of heaps of precious stones. There were diamonds there whose value the fisherman knew not – pearls larger than ever a diver had gathered – emeralds, sapphires and rubies, that would have made the jewellers of the world wonder; the merman then said:

'This is my eldest daughter's dowry.'

'Good luck attend her!' said Civil. 'It is the dowry of a queen.' But the merman led him on to another chamber: it was filled with heaps of gold coins, which seemed gathered from all times and nations. The images and inscriptions of all the kings that ever reigned were there; and the merman said:

'This is my second daughter's dowry.'

'Good luck attend her!' said Civil. 'It is a dowry for a princess.'

'So you may say,' replied the merman. 'But make up your mind which of the maidens you will marry, for the third has no portion at all, because she is not my daughter; but only, as you may see, a poor silly girl taken into my family for charity.'

'Truly, my lord,' said Civil, whose mind was already made up, 'both your daughters are too rich and far too noble for me; therefore I choose the third. Her poverty will best become my estate of a poor fisherman.'

'If you choose her,' said the merman, 'you must wait long for a wedding. I cannot allow an inferior girl to be married before my own daughters.' And he said a great deal more to dissuade him; but Civil would not change his mind, and they returned to the hall.

There was no more attention for the fisherman, but everybody watched him well. Turn where he would, master or guest had their eyes upon him, though he made them the best speeches he could remember, and praised all their splendours. One thing, however, was strange – there was no end to the fun and the feasting; nobody seemed tired, and nobody thought of sleep. When Civil's very eyes closed with weariness, and he slept on one of the marble benches no matter how many hours – there were the company feasting and dancing away; there were the thousand lamps within, and the cold moonlight without. Civil wished himself back with his mother, his net, and his cobbled skiff. Fishing would have been easier than those everlasting feasts; but there was nothing else among the sea people – no night of rest, no working day.

Civil knew not how time went on, till, waking up from a long sleep, he saw for the first time that the feast was over, and the company gone. The lamps still burned, and the tables, with all their riches, stood in the empty halls; but there was no face to be seen, no sound to be heard, only a low voice singing beside the outer door; and there, sitting all alone, he found the mild-eyed maiden.

'Fair lady,' said Civil, 'tell me what means this quietness, and where are all the merry company?'

'You are a man of the land,' said the lady, 'and know not the sea-people. They never sleep but once a year, and that is at Christmas time. Then they go into the deep caverns where there is always darkness, and sleep till the new year comes.'

'It is a strange fashion,' said Civil, 'but all folks have their way. Fair lady, as you and I are to be good friends, tell me, whence come all the wines and meats, and gold and silver vessels, seeing there are neither cornfields nor flocks here, workmen nor artificers?'

'The sea-people are heirs of the sea,' replied the maiden; 'to them come all the stores and riches that are lost in it. I know not the ways by which they come; but the lord of these halls keeps the keys of seven gates, where they go out and in; but one of the gates, which has not been open for thrice seven years, leads to a path under the sea, by which, I heard the merman say in his cups, one might reach the land. Good fisherman, if by chance you gain his favour, and ever open that gate, let me bear you company; for I was born where the sun shines and the grass grows, though my country and my parents are unknown to me. All I remember is sailing in a great ship, when a storm arose, and it was wrecked, and not one soul escaped drowning but me. I was then a little child, and a brave sailor had bound me to a floating plank before he was washed away. Here the sea-people came round me like great fishes, and I went down with them to this rich and weary country. Sometimes, as a great favour, they take me up with them to see the sun; but that is seldom, for they never like to part with one who has seen their country; and, fisherman, if you ever leave them, remember to take nothing with you that belongs to them, for if it were but a shell or a pebble, that will give them power over you and yours.'

'Thanks for your news, fair lady,' said Civil. 'A lord's daughter, doubtless, you must have been, while I am but a poor fisherman; yet, as we have fallen into the same misfortune, let us be friends, and it may be we shall find means to get back to the sunshine together.'

'You are a man of good manners,' said the lady, 'therefore, I accept your friendship; but my fear is that we shall never see the sunshine again.'

'Fair speeches brought me here,' said Civil, 'and fair speeches may help me back; but be sure I will not go without you.'

This promise cheered the lady's heart, and she and Civil spent that Christmas time seeing the wonders of the sea country. They wandered through caves like that of the great merman. The unfinished feast was spread in every hall; the tables were covered with most costly vessels; and heaps of jewels lay on the floors of unlocked chambers. But for the lady's warning, Civil would fain have put away some of them for his mother.

The poor woman was sad of heart by this time, believing her son to be drowned. On the first night when he did not come home, she had gone down to the sea and watched till morning. Then the fishermen steered out

89

again, and Sour having found his skiff floating about, brought it home, saying the foolish young man was doubtless lost; but what better could be expected when he had no discreet person to take care of him?

This grieved Dame Civil sore. She never expected to see her son again; but, feeling lonely in her cottage at the evening hour when he used to come home, the good woman accustomed herself to go down at sunset and sit beside the sea. That winter happened to be mild on the coast of the west country, and one evening when Christmas time was near, and the rest of the village preparing to make merry, Dame Civil sat as usual on the sands. The tide was ebbing and the sun going down, when from the eastward came a lady clad in black, mounted on a black palfrey, and followed by a squire in the same sad clothing; as the lady came near she said:

'Woe is me for my daughter, and for all that have lost by the sea!'

'You say well, noble lady,' said Dame Civil. 'Woe is me also for my son, for I have none beside him.'

When the lady heard that, she alighted from her palfrey and sat down by the fisherman's mother, saying:

'Listen to my story. I was the widow of a great lord in the heart of the east country. He left me a fair castle, and an only daughter, who was the joy of my heart. Her name was Faith Feignless; but, while she was yet a child, a great fortune-teller told me that my daughter would marry a fisherman. I thought this would be a great disgrace to my noble family, and therefore sent my daughter with her nurse in a good ship, bound for a certain city where my relations live, intending to follow myself as soon as I could get my lands and castles sold. But the ship was wrecked, and my daughter drowned; and I have wandered over the world with my good Squire Trusty, mourning on every shore with those who have lost friends by the sea. Some with whom I have mourned grew to forget their sorrow, and would lament with me no more; others being sour and selfish, mocked me, saying my grief was nothing to them: but you have good manners, and I will remain with you, however humble be your dwelling. My squire carries gold enough to pay all our charges.'

So the mourning lady and her good Squire Trusty went home with Dame Civil, and she was no longer lonely in her sorrow, for when the dame said:

'Oh, if my son were alive, I should never let him go to sea in a cobbled skiff!' the lady answered:

'Oh, if my daughter were but living, I should never think it a disgrace though she married a fisherman!'

The Christmas passed as it always does in the west country – shepherds made merry on the downs and fishermen on the shore; but when the merrymakings and ringing of bells were over in all the land, the sea-people woke up to their continual feasts and dances. Like one that had forgotten all that was past, the merman again showed Civil the chamber of gold and the chamber of jewels, advising him to choose between his two daughters; but the fisherman still answered that the ladies were too noble, and far too rich for him. Yet as he looked at the glittering heap, Civil could not help recollecting the poverty of the west country, and the thought slipped out:

'How happy my old neighbours would be to find themselves here!'

'Say you so?' said the merman, who always wanted visitors.

'Yes,' said Civil, 'I have neighbours up yonder in the west country whom it would be hard to send home again if they got sight of half this wealth;' and the honest fisherman thought of Dame Sour and her son.

The merman was greatly delighted with these speeches – he thought there was a probability of getting many land-people down, and by and by said to Civil:

'Suppose you took up a few jewels, and went up to tell your poor neighbours how welcome we might make them?'

The prospect of getting back to his country rejoiced Civil's heart, but he had promised not to go without the lady, and therefore answered prudently what was indeed true:

'Many thanks, my lord, for choosing such a humble man as I am to bear your message; but the people of the west country never believe anything without two witnesses at the least; yet if the poor maid whom I have chosen could be permitted to accompany me, I think they would believe us both.'

The merman said nothing in reply, but his people, who had heard Civil's speech, talked it over among themselves till they grew sure that the whole west country would come down if they only had news of the riches, and petitioned their lord to send up Civil and the poor maid by way of letting them know.

As it seemed for the public good, the great merman consented; but, being determined to have them back, he gathered out of his treasure

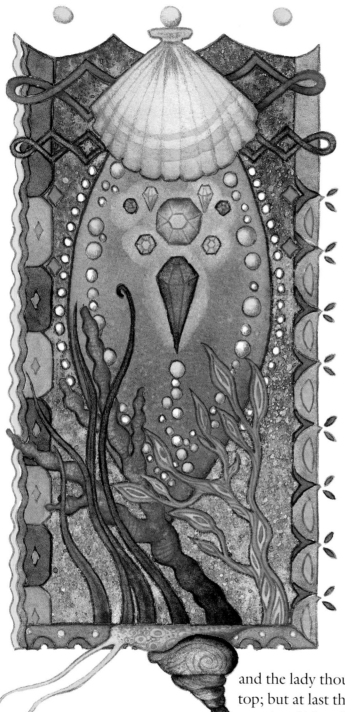

chamber some of the largest pearls and diamonds that lay convenient, and said:

'Take these as a present from me, to let the west country people see what I can do for my visitors.'

Civil and the lady took the presents, saying:

'Oh, my lord, you are too generous. We want nothing but the pleasure of telling of your marvellous riches up yonder.'

'Tell everybody to come down, and they will get the like,' said the merman; 'and follow my eldest daughter, for she carries the key of the land gate.'

Civil and the lady followed the mermaid through a winding gallery which led from the chief banquet hall far into the marble hill. All was dark, and they had neither lamp nor torch, but at the end of the gallery they came to a great stone gate, which creaked like thunder on its hinges. Beyond that there was a narrow cave, sloping up and up like a steep hillside. Civil and the lady thought they would never reach the top; but at last they saw a gleam of daylight, then a strip of blue sky, and the mermaid bade them stoop and creep through what seemed a crevice

in the ground, and both stood up on the broad sea-beach as the day was breaking and the tide ebbing fast away.

'Good times to you among your west country people,' said the mermaid. 'Tell any of them that would like to come down to visit us, that they must come here midway between the high and low water-mark, when the tide is going out at morning or evening. Call thrice on the sea-people, and we will show them the way.'

Before they could make answer, she had sunk down from their sight, and there was no track or passage there, but all was covered by the loose sand and sea-shells.

93

'Now,' said the lady to Civil, 'we have seen the heavens once more and we will not go back. Cast in the merman's present quickly before the sun rises;' and taking the bag of pearls and diamonds, she flung it as far as she could into the sea.

Civil never was so unwilling to part with anything as that bag, but he thought it better to follow a good example and tossed his into the sea also. They thought they heard a long moan come up from the waters; but Civil saw his mother's chimney beginning to smoke, and with the fair lady in her sea-green gown he hastened to the good dame's cottage.

The whole village were wakened that morning with cries of 'Welcome back, my son!' 'Welcome back, my daughter!' for the mournful lady knew it was her lost daughter, Faith Feignless, whom the fisherman had brought back, and all the neighbours assembled to hear their story. When it was told everybody praised Civil for the prudence he had shown in his difficulties, except Sour and his mother: they did nothing but rail upon him for losing such great chances of making himself and the whole country rich. At last, when they heard over and over again of the merman's treasures, neither mother nor son would consent to stay any longer in the west country, and as nobody dissuaded them, and they would not take Civil's direction, Sour got out his boat and steered away with his mother towards the Merman's Rock. From that voyage they never came back to the hamlet. Some say they went down and lived among the sea-people; others say – I know not how they learned it – that Sour and his mother grumbled and growled so much that even the sea-people grew weary of them and turned them and their boat out on the open sea. What part of the world they chose to land on nobody is certain: by all accounts they have been seen everywhere, and I should not be surprised if they were in this good company. As for Civil, he married Faith Feignless, and became a great lord.

Here the voice ceased, and two that were clad in sea-green silk, with coronets of pearls, rose up, and said:

'That's our story.'

'Oh, mamma, if we could get down to that country!' said Princess Greedalind.

'And bring all the treasures back with us!' answered Queen Wantall.

'Except the tale of yesterday, and the four that went before it, I have not heard such a story since my brother Wisewit went from me, and was lost in the forest,' said King·Winwealth. 'Readyrein, the second of my pages, rise and bring this maiden a purple velvet mantle.'

The mantle was brought, and Snowflower having thanked the king went down upon her grandmother's chair; but that night the little girl went no farther than the lowest banquet hall, where she was bidden to stay and share the feast, and sleep hard by in a wainscot chamber. That she was well entertained there is no doubt, for King Winwealth had been heard to say that it was not clear to him how he could have got through the seven days' feast without her grandmother's chair and its stories; but next day being the last of the seven, things were gayer than ever in the palace. The music had never been so merry, the dishes so rich, or the wines so rare; neither had the clamours at the gate ever been so loud, nor the disputes and envies so many in the halls.

Perhaps it was these doings that brought the low spirits earlier than usual on King Winwealth, for after dinner his majesty fell into them so deeply that a message came down from the highest banquet hall, and the cupbearer told Snowflower to go up with her chair, for King Winwealth wished to hear another story.

Now the little girl put on all her finery, from the pink shoes to the purple mantle, and went up with her chair, looking so like a princess that the whole company rose to welcome her. But having made her curtsy, and laid down her head, saying, 'Chair of my grandmother, tell me a story,' the clear voice from under the cushion answered:

'Listen to the story of Merrymind.'

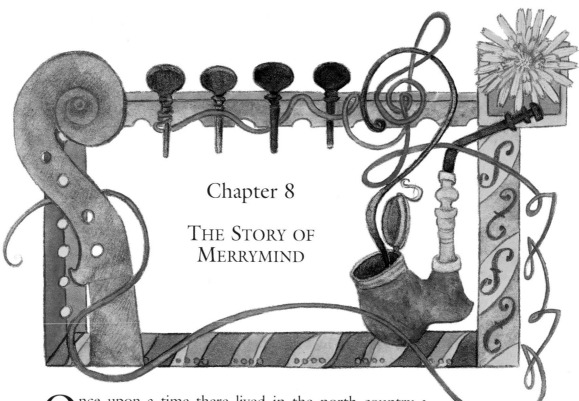

Chapter 8

THE STORY OF MERRYMIND

Once upon a time there lived in the north country a certain poor man and his wife, who had two cornfields, three cows, five sheep and thirteen children. Twelve of these children were called by names common in the north country – Hardhead, Stiffneck, Tightfingers and the like; but when the thirteenth came to be named, either the poor man and his wife could remember no other name, or something in the child's look made them think it proper, for they called him Merrymind, which the neighbours thought a strange name and very much above their station: however, as they showed no other signs of pride, the neighbours let that pass. Their thirteen children grew taller and stronger every year, and they had hard work to keep them in bread. But when the youngest was old enough to look after his father's sheep, there happened the great fair, to which everybody in the north country went, because it came only once in seven years, and was held on Midsummer Day – not in any town or village, but on a green plain, lying between a broad river and a high hill, where it was said the fairies used to dance in old and merry times.

Merchants and dealers of all sorts crowded to that fair from far and near. There was nothing known in the north country that could not be bought or sold in it, and neither old nor young were willing to go home without a fairing. The poor man who owned this large family could afford them little to spend in such ways; but as the fair happened only once in seven years, he would not show a poor spirit. Therefore, calling them about him, he opened the leathern bag in which his savings were stored and gave every one of the thirteen a silver penny.

The boys and girls had never before owned so much pocket-money; and, wondering what they should buy, they dressed themselves in their holiday clothes, and set out with their father and mother to the fair. When they came near the ground that midsummer morning, the stalls, heaped up with all manner of merchandise, from gingerbread upwards, the tents for fun and feasting, the puppet shows, the rope-dancers and the crowd of neighbours and strangers, all in their best attire, made those simple people think their north country fair the finest sight in the world. The day wore away in seeing wonders, and in chatting with old friends. It was surprising how far silver pennies went in those days; but before evening twelve of the thirteen had got fairly rid of their money. One bought a pair of brass buckles, another a crimson riband, a third green garters; the father bought a tobacco-pipe, the mother a horn snuffbox – in short, all had provided themselves with fairings except Merrymind.

The cause of the silver penny remaining in his pocket was that he had set his heart upon a fiddle; and fiddles enough there were in the fair – small and large, plain and painted. He looked at and priced the most of them, but there was not one that came within the compass of a silver penny. His father and mother warned him to make haste with his purchase, for they must all go home at sunset, because the way was long.

The sun was getting low and red upon the hill; the fair was growing thin, for many dealers had packed up their stalls and departed; but there was a mossy hollow in the great hillside, to which the outskirts of the fair had reached, and Merrymind thought he would see what might be there. The first thing was a stall of fiddles, kept by a young merchant from a far country, who had many customers, his goods being fine and new; but hard by sat a little grey-haired man, at whom everybody had laughed that day, because he had nothing on his stall but one old dingy fiddle, and all its strings were broken. Nevertheless the little man sat as stately, and cried 'Fiddles to sell!' as if he had the best stall in the fair.

'Buy a fiddle, my young master?' he said as Merrymind came forward. 'You shall have it cheap: I ask but a silver penny for it; and if the strings were mended, its like would not be in the north country.'

Merrymind thought this a great bargain. He was a handy boy and could mend the strings while watching his father's sheep. So down went the silver penny on the little man's stall and up went the fiddle under Merrymind's arm.

'Now, my young master,' said the little man, 'you see that we merchants have a deal to look after, and if you help me to bundle up my stall, I will tell you a wonderful piece of news about that fiddle.'

Merrymind was good-natured and fond of news, so he helped him to tie up with an old rope the loose boards and stocks that composed his stall, and when they were hoisted on his back like a faggot, the little man said:

'About that fiddle, my young master: it is certain the strings can never be mended nor made new, except by threads from the night-spinners, which, if you get, it will be a good pennyworth;' and up the hill he ran like a greyhound.

Merrymind thought that was queer news, but being given to hope the best, he believed the little man was only jesting, and made haste to join the rest of the family, who were soon on their way home. When they got there everyone showed his bargain, and Merrymind showed his fiddle; but his brothers and sisters laughed at him for buying such a thing when he had never learned to play. His sisters asked him what music he could bring out of broken strings; and his father said:

'Thou hast shown little prudence in laying out thy first penny, from which token I fear thou wilt never have many to lay out.'

In short, everybody threw scorn on Merrymind's bargain except his mother. She, good woman, said if he laid out one penny ill, he might lay out the next better; and who knew but his fiddle would be of use some day? To make her words good, Merrymind fell to repairing the strings – he spent all his time, both night and day, upon them; but, true to the little man's parting words, no mending would stand, and no string would hold on that fiddle. Merrymind tried everything and wearied himself to no purpose. At last he thought of inquiring after people who spun at night; and this seemed such a good joke to the north country people that they wanted no other till the next fair.

In the meantime Merrymind lost credit at home and abroad. Everybody believed in his father's prophecy; his brothers and sisters valued him no more than a herd boy; the neighbours thought he must turn out a scape-grace. Still the boy would not part with his fiddle. It was his silver pennyworth, and he had a strong hope of mending the strings for all that had come and gone; but since nobody at home cared for him except his mother, and as she had twelve other children, he resolved to leave the scorn behind him, and go to seek his fortune.

The family were not very sorry to hear of that intention, being in a manner ashamed of him; besides, they could spare one out of thirteen. His father gave him a barley cake, and his mother her blessing. All his brothers and sisters wished him well. Most of the neighbours hoped that no harm would happen to him; and Merrymind set out one summer morning with the broken-stringed fiddle under his arm.

There were no highways then in the north country – people took whatever path pleased them best; so Merrymind went over the fairground and up the hill, hoping to meet the little man and learn something of the night-spinners. The hill was covered with heather to the top, and he went up without meeting anyone. On the other side it was steep and rocky, and after a hard scramble down, he came to a narrow glen all overgrown with wild furze and brambles. Merrymind had never met with briars so sharp, but he was not the boy to turn back readily, and pressed on in spite of torn clothes and scratched hands, till he came to the end of the glen, where two paths met: one of them wound through a pine wood, he knew not how far, but it seemed green and pleasant. The other was a rough, stony way leading to a wide valley surrounded by high hills and overhung by a dull thick mist, though it was yet early in the summer evening.

Merrymind was weary with his long journey, and stood thinking of what path to choose, when by the way of the valley there came an old man as tall and large as any three men of the north country. His white hair and beard hung like tangled flax about him; his clothes were made of sackcloth; and on his back he carried a heavy burden of dust heaped high in a great pannier.

'Listen to me, you lazy vagabond!' he said, coming near to Merrymind. 'If you take the way through the wood I know not what will happen to you; but if you choose this path you must help me with my pannier, and I can tell you it's no trifle.'

'Well, father,' said Merrymind, 'you seem tired, and I am younger than you, though not quite so tall; so, if you please, I will choose this way and help you along with the pannier.'

Scarce had he spoken when the huge man caught hold of him, firmly bound one side of the pannier to his shoulders with the same strong rope that fastened it on his own back, and never ceased scolding and calling him names as they marched over the stony ground together. It was a rough way and a heavy burden, and Merrymind wished himself a thousand times out of the old man's company, but there was no getting off; and at length, in hopes of beguiling the way and putting him in better humour, he began to sing an old rhyme which his mother had taught him. By this time they had entered the valley, and the night had fallen very dark and cold. The old man ceased scolding, and by a feeble glimmer of the moonlight, which now began to shine, Merrymind saw that they were close by a deserted cottage, for its door stood open to the night winds. Here the old man paused, and loosed the rope from his own and Merrymind's shoulders.

'For seven times seven years,' he said, 'have I carried this pannier, and no one ever sang while helping me before. Night releases all men, so I release you. Where will you sleep – by my kitchen fire, or in that cold cottage?'

Merrymind thought he had got quite enough of the old man's society, and therefore answered:

'The cottage, good father, if you please.'

'A sound sleep to you then!' said the old man, and he went off with his pannier.

Merrymind stepped into the deserted cottage. The moon was shining through door and window, for the mist was gone, and the night looked clear as day; but in all the valley he could hear no sound, nor was there any trace of inhabitants in the cottage. The hearth looked as if there had not been a fire there for years. A single article of furniture was not to be seen; but Merrymind was sore weary, and laying himself down in a corner, with his fiddle close by, he fell fast asleep.

The floor was hard, and his clothes were thin, but all through his sleep there came a sweet sound of singing voices and spinning-wheels, and